Pl

Shadows on the Lake

Catherine Sefton is the pen name of Martin Waddell. He has written many books for children of all ages. He has won a number of awards including the the Smarties Prize, the Kurt Maschler Award, the Other Award and was a runner-up for the *Guardian* Children's Fiction Prize. He lives by the sea in Northern Ireland with his wife, three sons and their dog, Bessie.

Shadows
on the Lake

Catherine Sefton

PUFFIN BOOKS

For Mark and Sarah

PUFFIN BOOKS

Published by the Penguin Group
Penguin Books Ltd, 27 Wrights Lane, London W8 5TZ, England
Penguin Books USA Inc., 375 Hudson Street, New York, New York 10014, USA
Penguin Books Australia Ltd, Ringwood, Victoria, Australia
Penguin Books Canada Ltd, 10 Alcorn Avenue, Toronto, Ontario, Canada M4V 3B2
Penguin Books (NZ) Ltd, 182–190 Wairau Road, Auckland 10, New Zealand

Penguin Books Ltd, Registered Offices: Harmondsworth, Middlesex, England

First published by Hamish Hamilton Ltd 1987
Published in Puffin Books 1995
1 3 5 7 9 10 8 6 4 2

Made and printed in Great Britain by Clays Ltd, St Ives plc

"If we find the stuff, we can challenge Baxter with it, and tell him we'll go to the police if he doesn't stop stealing," I said.

"If he is stealing," Peter said.

"If he is," I said.

It felt like a betrayal.

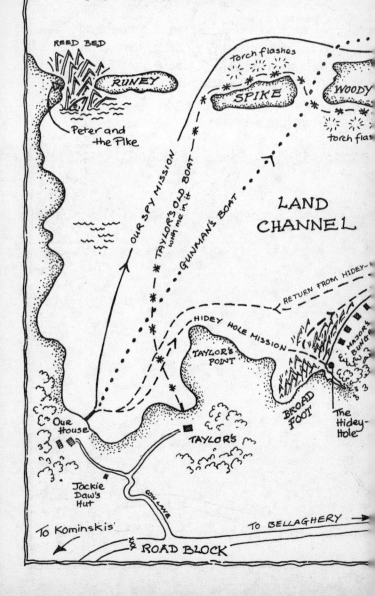

GUNMAN'S BOAT

TAYLOR'S
OLD BOAT
(with me in it)
LANDING POINT

Round
Tower
V/A

GUNMAN'S
BOAT
LANDING
POINT

■ Vault

Ruins ■ Tin Hut

HOLY
ISLAND

SPY
MISSION
LANDING
POINT

BAILIFF'S
ROCKS

OUR SPY MISSION

REED
CHANNEL

N

MAJOR'S
HOUSE

MAJOR'S LAKE

HOTEL Pier

BELLAGHERY

1

My name is Annie Orr and I'm thirteen and a bit, which is too young to be mixed up in kidnapping and blue murder and men with guns and nightmares out on an old dark lake, but that is what happened to me.

It began with me and the Squirt getting off the bus at the top of Cow Lane. The Squirt is my brother, Peter. I am the middle one in the family, and my other brother Baxter is the eldest.

I'm supposed to look after the Squirt. It takes some doing.

"Are you not going to carry a bag for me, Squirt?" I said, because I was laden down with the shopping. I get most of the shopping and things to do, since my mother died. They all treat me like their slave, or they'd like to, and I was in no mind to do all their humping for them.

I put the bags down in the lane, and he picked one up. It was the small one, with the bread and lettuce in it.

"You're not going to strain a muscle, then," I told him.

"I'm saving my strength for fishing," he said.

"Big deal!" I told him. It is not as if he ever

catches much you could eat, though he tries hard enough. He goes on about some big pike he is after down the reed bed at Runey, but he is never likely to catch it, for I think it sees him coming. My Dad and Baxter have both been out on the lake after it, as well as nearly everybody else round Bellaghery, and if they can't nab it I see precious little chance of Peter doing the job.

"The big pike would eat you alive if it caught on your line!" I told him, and we started off down the lane, with me carrying the heavy bag and the fisherman doing his dance with the bread and lettuce. He was hopping on and off the ditches like a kangaroo.

I was exhausted, just watching him.

The usual happened; he took one of his big leaps and missed, grabbed out a hand at the brambles and ended up in the ditch. It was the ditch round the side of the Taylors' back field, the *drain* ditch.

"Oh heck!" he said, standing up, and sinking deeper.

"You can wash those yourself!" I told him, looking at his jeans.

He sloshed out, with the black mud dripping off him.

"Walk well away from me, for you're no perfume garden!" I said.

Then I spotted the bread and lettuce, and the white bag, which was sinking down into the ooze.

"You get right back down in the ditch and fish that out!" I said, but when he got it out I knew he needn't have bothered.

"You may drop it back in," I said, when he handed me the soggy bundle.

"It would dry out," he said.

"You eat it," I said. "I'm not!"

"Well, we'll have to get some more," Peter said.

"What with?" I said, sourly.

"Money," he said.

I could have told him I was the one who had to do the house-keeping money, but I didn't. I gave him his drippy bag back and went on down the lane.

"I'll use it for ground bait if we can't eat it," he said, squelching after me. The mud was all down his jeans, and his baseball boots were covered in it. The Squirt is a mess at the best of times. He has grown his hair long since my Mum died. She'd never have let him go around shaggy like that in his old jeans and denim jacket, but my Dad pays no heed to anyone's appearance, these days.

By the time we came to the house, I'd made a big decision.

"You're not coming in here like that, Squirt," I told him.

"Says who?" he said.

"Says me," I said. "You'll dirty my clean floor. Go throw yourself in the lake."

"Good idea," he said and off he went. I dumped the bag in the house and went after him.

When I got there the Squirt was up to his waist in the water by our landing stage, mucky jeans and all.

"It's better than a bath!" he said. "Are you not coming in?"

I wished I was, because the lake was flat and silky and shiny, with not a ripple on it, and I was a boiled egg from bag-carrying, but I hadn't time.

"I've got to get Baxter's tea ready," I said.

"No, you haven't," he said.

"Why not?"

"Because Baxter is away off in the boat," he said.

"What boat?" I said, with a sinking feeling inside me. I knew it wasn't our boat, because our boat was tied up by the post, rocking gently on the water.

"Marky Taylor's," he said.

"Oh," I said.

"So you might as well have a swim," he said.

"Yes," I said. "I'll go and get my costume."

I went back to the house, glad for a chance to get away from Peter. I didn't want him to see what I was thinking, and the Squirt is sharp about things like that.

Baxter out on the lake with Marky Taylor!

The Taylors are round the lane from us. They have the grazing on our bit of the lake, as far as the Broadfoot, and they are shifty people. It was Marky Taylor who got Baxter into trouble about the bicycles. My Dad was mad about it, because we've never had the police coming to our house before, and it was just too much, coming a month after my Mum dying. Baxter had to go to court in Squiresbridge. My Dad went round to the Taylors' breathing fire and brimstone and he told them what he thought of them, and how he didn't want to see Marky about the place again. Old Taylor called my Dad names, and for months none of them spoke to any of us, which was no harm done.

My Dad told Baxter he'd skin him alive if he got in any more trouble, and made him promise not to go near the Taylors.

That was all fine, if you could call it fine, as far as it went, but it didn't go far. I knew sooner or later he would get mixed up with Marky again, because the Taylors are our next-door neighbours, if you count round their point as next door, and there was nobody else to talk to. Our house is a good way from the rest of the world, down Cow Lane. There are only three houses at the bottom of the lane, ours and the Taylors' and Jackie Daw's hut, and Jackie's doesn't count because it is hardly a house at all. Jackie has a screw loose in the head. You could hardly expect Baxter to get all pally with him when Jackie spends his time rooting through other people's rubbish and hiding what he finds away in bags like a jackdaw.

Now Baxter was off in the boat with Marky. If my father got word of it there would be a big row, and muggins would be caught in the middle. Not because the row would be anything to do with me, but because I always am caught between them when they have goes at each other. I'm the only other grown-up around. Well, *almost* grown up.

I changed and came back down by the lake. Peter was laying flat out in our boat, shielding his eyes from the sun. The sun was beaming down, and the water was lapping the jetty posts.

I took a run off the end of the jetty, and dive-bombed in.

It was great in the water, just floating around. I lay on my back and let it lap over me, all golden and peaty.

I would have been happy, if it wasn't for Baxter.

"Where's our engine?" the Squirt said, sitting up in the boat.

"Baxter must have taken it," I said. "I wonder where they've gone?"

The Taylors have a mucky old boat with a squeaky Bluebird engine that keeps going phut so that they have to row home. It makes no difference if you're only out on our bit of the lake, like Peter after his pike, but anyone going any distance would be a fool to trust it.

So they weren't just fishing. That was no surprise really, because I'd checked Baxter's fishing things in the shed when I went back to the house to change, and they were all there.

"Same place they always go," the Squirt said, replying to my question.

Always? It was the first I'd heard of it.

"Have they been going out a lot, then?" I said.

"Yes," Peter said, standing up on the boat so that it wobbled.

"Where to?"

"They mozey off to the island, or somewhere," he said. "Up the far end, beyond Bellaghery."

"Holy Island?" I said, surprised, because Holy Island is a fair way off, and there's nothing much on it when you get there, barring a few ruins, a tin hut and a round tower. Nothing much to interest the likes of Marky Taylor, anyway.

"Dunno," said Peter, climbing out onto the jetty. "Baxter isn't telling. He said he'd give me a thick ear if I didn't mind my own business."

"You asked him?" I said.

Asking Baxter what he doesn't want to tell you can be a risky business. Since he began having arguments with my Dad, Baxter has got a lot snappier to live with.

"I didn't mean to ask him, till he caught me," Peter said, sounding a bit awkward.

"Caught you doing what, Squirt?"

"I was down at the Point one night, when they came in," he said. "I have as much right down the Point as anyone, haven't I?"

"Spying on Baxter!" I said.

"Well, sort of," he admitted.

There was an awkward silence.

"Don't!" I said.

"Don't what?"

"Don't do it again," I said.

The Squirt didn't say anything. He just hoofed it off to the house.

I got out of the water, and sat with my feet over the end of the jetty. If the Squirt had got his piggy nose into it, there must be something going on, and I hadn't even noticed. I wonder how often Baxter had been out in the boat with Marky Taylor, and what they could be doing at the island. I wonder if I even wanted to know. Knowing could only be trouble.

But not knowing might mean trouble too, if my Dad caught on that something was happening.

I didn't want there to be any more trouble for my Dad, or Baxter, or any of us.

My first thought was that I would face Baxter out, and tell him whatever it was he was mixed up in with the Taylor family he was to stop it, because the Taylors are a bad lot, and it is only luck that has kept them out of prison so far.

I couldn't see myself saying a thing like that to Baxter.

In the end, I decided to let well alone.

2

I would have let well alone, but for what happened two days later, down at Bellaghery Pier.

My Dad and Baxter work down at Bellaghery, for Miles Sharry. My Dad has a real job, helping out with Miles' cruisers that he lets out on the lake, and Baxter has a pretend one, giving a hand with the bar in Sharry's hotel. Miles hasn't got Baxter on the business books, he just slips him a few pounds now and then, and no questions asked by the taxman or the insurance or anybody. Baxter shouldn't do it, but what else *can* he do, for there is no work in Bellaghery or anywhere else round here, and nobody can live on the dole.

Anyway, I went down to the pier to see if my Dad was there, and he wasn't, but Marky Taylor was, and our Peter was with him.

I wasn't too happy about that, but I wouldn't have interfered, if Marky hadn't lost his temper.

He started belting Peter!

Peter yelled and fell over the ropes, and then he started scrambling away, but Marky was after him swinging his fists.

I headed bang into the row.

"You stop that this minute, Marky Taylor, or

I'll have my Dad on you!" I shouted, and I grabbed hold of Peter.

"Tell that wee skitter to keep out of my road!" Marky shouted.

"You have no call to thump anyone his size!" I said.

"Don't you let him near me again!" Marky said. "Tell him to keep his snout out of my business."

For a moment I thought he was going to take a swing at me, too, and so did Peter. Peter was up on his feet. He came in between us and I think he would have had more trouble than he could cope with, only I grabbed at him.

"You know what you are, Marky Taylor?" I yelled, and I called him a name. I was glad my Dad didn't hear me calling names like that, but at the time I shouted it I didn't care, I just wanted to tell him he was the worst thing I could think of.

Even Marky was surprised.

"Away and wash your mouth out with soap, Annie Orr!" he said, and he grumped off.

I watched him go down the pier, and then I turned back to Peter.

"You all right, Squirt?" I said.

"Yes, thanks," Peter said.

Marky had really scared him. There's no way the Squirt would thank me for anything, in the normal way of going, but this time it was different.

"I'm going to find Dad," I said. "He'll sort that Marky one out."

"No," Peter said.

"Why no?"

"Because," Peter said.

"Because *what*?" I said, getting irritated, and suspicious at the same time.

"Because I don't want Dad to know," the Squirt said. "Right?"

"Not right at all," I said.

"I was having a snoop," Peter said. "You know, round the Taylors' boat, and Marky came back from the hotel and he caught me. And I don't want Dad knowing, see? Because he'd only want to know what I was snooping *for*."

"What were you snooping for?" I said.

"I don't want to say," Peter said.

He wouldn't budge, either, though I kept at him. The Squirt is like that. Once he has an idea in his head, he will stick to it, and whatever his idea was I wasn't part of it.

"Listen, Peter," I said. "This is about Baxter, isn't it? Our brother, and his goings on. That's what you were snooping into?"

No reply.

"You're not to do it, do you hear? And you're not to get mixed up with the likes of Marky Taylor and his dealings, even if Baxter is. I'm telling you."

"And I'm not listening," he said.

"Okay," I said. "I'll tell Dad, and he can sort it out."

"Don't," he said.

"Why shouldn't I?"

"Please, *don't*, Annie," he said.

"I'll have to think about it," I said. "But for now you stay away from the Taylors and Baxter, okay?"

He didn't say it was okay, and he didn't say it wasn't.

I went off up the pier feeling really mad at him, and mad at Baxter was well. The Squirt's snooping would only make things worse; they'd both end up in trouble.

I'll have it out with Baxter! I decided, and I headed off for the hotel, but when I got there Baxter wasn't available. He was at Allie Sharry's car, helping her with her parcels. Allie is the daughter of Old Baldy Miles Sharry, and there is no way on God's earth that she is going to take a sudden passion for our Baxter, but he doesn't know that. By the way he was lugging her parcels for her and trying to smooch up to her at the same time, he was certainly trying.

It was disgusting.

I waited round to see if she would clear off, but the pair of them stayed chatting by the car like two love-birds. They'd be at it still, if old Baldy hadn't popped out of the hotel, all gold wristwatch and flashy suit, yelling for Baxter.

That cut off the lovey-dovey stuff.

Allie Sharry tossed her hair and flounced away, leaving Baxter to get the rough edge of Miles Sharry's tongue. I felt really sorry for him. Baxter is tall and lean and brown, and loose-limbed, like a cowboy, and Miles is short and fat and bald and rich and bossy. Whatever he was saying to Baxter, he didn't mince his words. I could see Baxter's chin setting, but there was nothing he could do about it.

Miles Sharry has our whole family over a barrel. He owns our house, down by the lake, and we only get to live there because my Dad works for him. We wouldn't have it if he could fill it full of tourists, but with the troubles in Northern Ireland there are no tourists. The house goes with the job, but once he had us in it Miles made the most of his advantage. My Dad hasn't had a rise in ages, and Miles only pays Baxter peanuts, and he knows that neither of them can say a word because if they lose their jobs, they lose our house as well. It is really wicked.

Miles stalked off, leaving a cloud of aftershave behind him, and Baxter hurried back into the hotel. I didn't go after him. It wasn't the time for a confrontation.

Instead I started up the street, and there was Peter sitting on the wall.

He looked just like Baxter only smaller and hairier. He was watching me, as I came up to him, with that clever look on him. I sometimes think Peter is smarter than the rest of us put together.

"Hi, Bossy boots!" he said, swinging down off the wall. "Did you tell him then?"

"No," I said.

"Good," he said.

"I'm worried about you getting into trouble as well as Baxter," I said.

"You treat me like a little kid, Annie," he said. "Come off it! I'm almost the same age as you."

He was right. He's twelve and a bit. It's just that he stayed small in size, long after I shot up. That's when we began calling him the Squirt, and thinking he was small, because he looked it. Now he's started putting on height, he looks more his real age.

"You can't baby me any more," he said.

"Okay, I won't," I said.

"Good," he said. "So what are *we* going to do about Baxter?"

I'd been thinking about that, while I was watching Baxter and his sweetie-pie at the hotel. Peter was right to snoop, because trouble for Baxter meant trouble for all of us. He was right, and it was up to me to help him.

"Do?" I said. "It's summer, isn't it? And we are supposed to be on our school holidays, even if there is precious little holiday about it as far as I'm concerned. We'll do what other people do on their holidays."

"What's that?" he said.

14

"We'll take our boat out on the lake," I said. "Round Runey and Spike and Woody and the reed channel, as far as Holy Island. And then we might land, to stretch our legs . . . "

"*Just* to stretch our legs?" he said.

For a kid, the Squirt catches on quick.

"Bearing in mind that our eyes walk around on top of our stretched legs, with just a bit of head and body in between," I said.

"And there's no reason why we should keep our eyes shut when we're out there!" Squirt said.

He was getting excited, and that worried me. Sometimes he is sensible, but not when he gets big ideas.

"Expedition Rules," I said. "I'm in charge, because I'm the eldest and what I say goes, right?"

"Wrong," he said.

"Why wrong?"

"Wrong because you don't know what we're looking for, and I *think* I do," he said.

"What?"

"That's the same question you asked me before, and I'm still not telling you," he said, annoyingly.

"I thought this was supposed to be a joint operation, to keep Baxter out of trouble?" I said. "What about pooling information."

"You haven't got any information to pool," he said. "And I don't want to tell you what I think, in case I'm wrong, and then I'd look silly."

I started to argue, but then I didn't. It was funny. Peter had always been the Squirt, someone I could boss about, but now he was beginning to change. Maybe he was fed up with being bossed, and determined to make sure that it didn't happen any more.

"Okay," I said. "But I'm still in charge of the operation, agreed?"

"Why?" he said.

"Because I *am* older than you are, even if you like to think I'm not, and because everybody thinks you are daft and thinks I am sensible, and that means I'll be the one who gets into trouble if things go wrong!" I said.

He thought for a bit, and then he said: "All right! You're on!"

3

We couldn't just go back to our house and get out the boat and buzz off to the island because I *wasn't* on holidays, even though I am supposed to be. I have a job.

I am on the Black Economy, at Kominskis'.

The Kominskis are Hungarian refugees who landed up in Northern Ireland at the time of the Hungarian Revolution, in the 1950s. Lazlo got work at the shipyard in Belfast and then he was made redundant early and he and Petra, his wife, used the redundancy money to buy up the old house at Wheeler's Mill from Miles Sharry. They pulled a fast one on old Baldy Gold Pants Sharry, for once they had the place they opened up a Continental Restaurant selling fancy Hungarian food to the tourists. Nobody thought they would make a go of it but they did, and now I am a part-time Continental Cookery Assistant and Waitress in the school holidays, and I get eight pounds a week most weeks, and twelve if there is a rush of people and I have to do longer hours. It is illegal employing me, but nobody minds.

I wasn't able to go off with Peter to the lake straight away, because I had to do my work and then when I'd done all I was supposed to do, there was a complication. That's my life, one big complication.

This time it was Petra and her food bag.

Not for us. For old Jackie Daw.

I sometimes wonder how the Kominskis make any money, for there are times when you would think they are feeding half the countryside.

I had packed up, and was ready to nip off back down to the lake, when Petra called me.

"Hold on a minute," she said. "I have a bag for Jackie."

She went into the kitchen to fill it up and just then didn't Lazlo come back from Bellaghery with some tourists. They were staying round the Point from us, across the Broadfoot in the Major's holiday bungalows, and the usual had happened: somebody had been in and pinched something.

Visitors getting their things pinched would be no business of mine but Lazlo and Petra are protective about Bellaghery, as if they had adopted the place, which I suppose they have in a way . . . I've never known such people for taking other people's troubles on.

Lazlo had Petra out of the kitchen, and they went into their act.

I was left waiting for Jackie Daw's bag.

I could have filled it myself, but I wasn't easy in my mind about taking food from the kitchen, when I didn't know what Petra would call spare, and what she needed.

18

By the time I got away I was late, and then I had to make a detour round by Jackie's hut.

He wasn't in or, if he was, he didn't come out.

That would be like Jackie. He is shy of people.

I put the bag against the door, with a stone to stop animals getting it, and then I went off back to our house, got my anorak, and I headed down to the boat.

"What kept you?" Squirt asked.

"I came as quickly as I could," I told him, and then I spotted something else. "Where's the engine?" I asked.

Peter made a face.

"Baxter never brought it back from the Taylors'?" I said.

"Right!" said Peter, and he looked me in the eye. "Shall I go get it?" he said.

The same thought was in both our minds. Peter could end up with his block knocked off if he turned up at Marky's house asking for the engine, even if it was ours. I didn't exactly fancy another interview with Marky myself.

"No," I said, coming to a decision in my Leader-of-the-Expedition hat. "We'll row."

Brilliant idea!

The wind turned out to be against us. *And* the water was choppy, splattering the end of the boat.

I'd had the bright notion that we would go out between Runey Islands and Spike and let the flow carry us down the main channel, past

Woody and beyond Holy, where we would drift in and land amongst the reeds. The idea was that if anybody saw us, like the Taylors or Baxter, it wouldn't look as if we were going to Holy at all, just drifting around looking for fish.

It wasn't all that bright a notion, because the truth of the matter was that with the wind against us there *was* no drift.

We had to pull hard the whole way, taking it in turns to row or look after our by-the-way fishing tackle, even though we weren't fishing. It wasn't so bad in the shallows between Runey and Spike and Woody Islands, but there's a channel running down between Woody and Holy towards the pier at Bellaghery which is deep and swirly at the best of times, and it picked that evening to have a real battle with us when we started to cross it.

"Could we not go down towards Bellaghery with the flow and work our way round the back of the island through the reed channel?" Squirt asked me, leaning on the oars, after he'd been struggling with the current for about ten minutes, and making little or no headway.

"No," I said

"Why not?" he said.

"Because Dad might see us, dummy," I said.

Whatever we were about to find out . . . *if* we were about to find out *anything* . . . I didn't want Dad to know about it. I wanted to find out, and then we'd both go to Baxter and tell him to stop it, whatever it was, and then . . . and then . . . I wasn't too clear in my mind about the 'and then', but I was prepared to face it when I came to it. For now, I just wanted to be sure that my Dad had no whisper of anything odd going on.

"Look, Annie," Peter said, dropping his oars again. "We're going down towards Bellaghery and in round the reed channel or we're not going at all, for there is no way I will get her across in all this blow."

I had to give in, because he was right. There was no way we could manage the boat against the current, even if we'd taken an oar each.

I sat in the boat trying to look like somebody else, hoping all the while that Dad wouldn't spot us. I made the Squirt go right round the reed channel, away from the landing point opposite Bellaghery that everybody uses, and up the far side.

"Where do we go in?" he said.

"Give me the oars, and I'll show you," I said, and soon I had us pushing in through the reeds to the old broken-down stone jetty.

"How did you know about this?" he said, skipping out onto it.

"I'm an expert on islands!" I told him, but I didn't tell him that my expertise was only one row out with Anna Marie Carrig in her Dad's old boat, when we found the hidden jetty. Still, it made me look good, and reinforced the bit about

21

being Leader-in-Charge of the Expedition, which was beginning to sound hollow, considering we hadn't been able to follow the course I had set.

The trouble was, the journey had taken us ages and ages longer than we had planned. It was already getting dark.

It is a queer place, Holy Island, when you are on it at dusk, even if you do have your just-beginning-to-come-out-of-the-egg brother with you.

Spooky.

We headed off in the general direction of the ruins, up by the round tower. There's a tin hut and three old buildings that used to be an oratory and a chapel and something else, but that is not where the old monks lived. They had wooden buildings that Miss McCann taught us about in school, and she did us a map of how it might have been, and we all had to draw pictures of monks doing things. Then she gave us a whole history of the McSorley family who are buried in a fancy vault out there. The last one got hung and the family was ruined, and the only bit of their estates they had left when the Government finished with them was their old vault, stuffed full of dead ones. She started showing us the land the McSorleys owned before the English Government got them, and the way it sounded to me there wasn't much difference between them and our old Money Bags Gold

22

Pants Baldy Sharry, for all they were supposed to be so grand. They had a great time giving the peasantry hell and living off other people's labour, which is just what Miles Sharry does to us, trapped in our tourist house that he can't let.

For all Miss McCann's talk about the island belonging to us, both sides, Protestant and Catholic, because of what it stood for in Irish History, I don't believe her.

It is the old dead McSorleys' place really.

That's what I felt, anyway, walking round with the Squirt in the dusk.

I don't know what the Squirt thought we would find, but we didn't find it.

We just got colder and snifflier and the dark came down and suddenly the trees and the old ruins all seemed to be closing in around us. I had the feeling that whoever or whatever there was about the island wanted us off it.

It wasn't a nice feeling. It was horrid.

Neither one of us wanted to be the one who'd say "Let's go, because I'm scared". We were too grown up for that, but both of us wanted to go. In the end, I gave in.

"As official Leader of the Expedition I'm fed up and I want to go home," I said.

"Right," Squirt said.

Then we couldn't find the boat. We were poking about among the reeds for ages, trying to find the landing stage in the dark. We found it in the end, and wasted no time getting off the spooky old island.

The lake was just as spooky. The dark waters would give you the shudders, sometimes. They would give you the shudders another way, if you fell in!

"We're going to be late," Peter said. "There'll be One Mad Dad in the kitchen."

"Maybe there won't be," I said, not very hopefully.

"Altogether, our Big Spy Mission to sort brother Baxter hasn't been a success!" grumbled Peter.

I thought he was right.

No sign of Baxter or Dad when we got back to the house, which was lucky. Miles must have got them working overtime.

I went up to my own room, to be out of the way if they turned up and started another one of their rows. If I was up when the first one came in, I would end up making cups of tea. They have me elected tea lady in our house, and I had no mind to do it.

Instead, I sat by my window wondering, and looking out at the lake. I was looking out towards Runey Island. Beyond Runey lies Spike, and beyond Spike lies Woody and the Bailiffs Rocks and the Bellaghery Channel, where my Spy Mission plan had gone wrong because of the current, and beyond that again lies Holy Island, with the round tower and the ruined churches and the old dead McSorleys in their vault, who are not the folk I would choose for company in the moonlight.

We'd found nothing on the island.

Did that mean that there was nothing to find?

4

I was up before any of them the next morning, down first as usual because I have work to do and can't lie in my bed like some people.

My Dad and Peter were down next, and I made them their breakfasts. Dad was taking Peter on down to Squirestown to get the new rod he was so fussed about, then he'd drive back to Bellaghery, leaving Peter to thumb his way home. That left only the Sleepy Prince, taking a lie in because it wasn't one of his days for working at the hotel.

Baxter came down half an hour later and asked for his breakfast. I told him he could make his own.

"I'm not your paid servant, Baxter!" I told him.

He wasn't one bit pleased.

He burnt himself some bacon and went back off upstairs, leaving the kitchen reeking of cooking fat. I opened up the windows, and headed for the washing-line in the barn.

The next thing I heard was a car coming down the lane.

Somebody for the Taylors, I thought, out to buy some of their home brew. They do a bit of poteen distilling on the quiet, or they did, before the police caught up with them. Poteen is old raw gut alcohol. They were brewing it any which way, and selling it to Miles Sharry. He got rid of it under the counter at the hotel to the tourists, to blow their tiny minds. As usual, Miles didn't get caught out, but the Taylors did.

Another possibility was that it was the Welfare woman after Jackie. The Welfare woman tried putting Jackie into a home, but every time he went in Jackie broke out again, back to his collection of treasures picked out of everybody's bins. There isn't a dump in the land that is safe from Jackie and his black sacks. When the woman from the Welfare comes Jackie hides himself away somewhere, like his treasures, and he doesn't come out until she has gone.

But the car wasn't for Jackie, or the Taylors. It pulled past Taylors' turnoff and came round the bend to us. It pulled up outside our house and Sergeant Joe McDowell of the RUC got out, all dolled up in his flak jacket to stop the IRA from shooting him. The RUC is our police force. It stands for 'Royal Ulster Constabulary'.

My heart went right up into my mouth.

There is only one person they'd be after in our house.

Baxter.

His name is on their books after the bicycle business, although at the time Baxter didn't know that he was doing wrong. He was only

27

fixing up bikes with Marky Taylor so that Marky could re-sell them. He didn't know where Marky was getting the bikes from. It was Marky Taylor got him into trouble and the police know that; Joe McDowell said as much to my Dad.

What had the Taylors got him into this time? It looked as if all our secret missions to Holy Island were too late.

"Annie Orr?" Joe said.

"Yes," I said, coming out of the barn. He must have sharp eyes, for I'd thought I was out of the way. The idea in my head was that by staying out of the way but around the place I would learn what was going on, but Joe McDowell was too smart for me. I suppose that that is how he got to be a sergeant and not just an ordinary policeman standing on a street corner waiting to be blown up.

"Anybody about?" he said.

"Baxter's in the house," I said, and then I wished I hadn't said it, for it sounded as if I was expecting him to ask for Baxter, and not somebody else.

"Is your Dad about?" he said.

"My Dad has gone down to Squirestown, but he'll be back up to the pier, later," I told him, puzzled a bit, because I was certain sure it was Baxter he was after.

"It had better be Baxter then," he said.

That was the moment when Baxter came clattering out, looking worried.

"Good morning, Baxter," said Joe.

Baxter muttered something at him.

Sergeant Joe took a long look at the car. He had a police constable at the wheel, a man I've never seen round here before, and two more men in plain clothes in the back. One of them made a sign to Joe out of the window.

"Could I have a word with you in the house, Baxter?" the Sergeant said, and he half nodded in my direction, and then winked.

"Oh . . . aye!" Baxter said, catching on.

I was left marooned and out of it, as usual. I did let it cross my mind that I might go in and put the kettle on for the sergeant, but I had a notion that I might be turfed out on my ear.

Baxter took him into the kitchen, and that is the last I heard of any conversation. I could hardly go sneaking round the back to the window with a car load of cops looking on, could I?

They didn't stay put, either. The minute Baxter and the sergeant were inside the two plain clothes ones hopped out of the back of the car. One headed for the shed, and one headed for the barn.

I just gaped at them.

They were in and out dead quick, and then off into the bushes before I could get my brain straight about search warrants, and things. I couldn't see myself walking up and challenging them anyway. They moved around the bushes very casual, sort of, but from the flick of their eyes there was nothing casual about what they were doing.

I expected Baxter to come out in handcuffs, and be driven off to the station, and I was busy going over in my mind that I'd have to go down to the pier and break the news to my Dad.

Sergeant Joe came out of the house with Baxter with him, but apparently un-arrested, though he looked pale and his fingers were playing with the fraying collar of his shirt. He was walking on eggs!

"It's you, isn't it?" I said, rounding on him when the police car had gone off. "What have you done this time? Is it more stolen bicycles?"

"Mind your tongue, Annie Orr!" Baxter said, irritably.

"I hope you had it well hid, whatever it is!" I said. "For they searched the whole place while you were in there with the sergeant."

"They would do that," Baxter said, and he turned back to the house. I went after him, firing questions like a machine gun.

"I've nothing to say to you at all, Annie Orr!" Baxter snapped at me, and then he headed off upstairs to the bathroom, where I couldn't follow him.

He was no sooner out of the way, than Love's Young Dream came a-calling!

It was Allie Sharry, all auburn hair and soft eyes, a glorious blaze of white in her jeans and shirt, with a silk scarf on her that must have cost a bomb and a whiff of perfume you could tame lions with, if you had a lion to tame.

"There's a young lady to see you, Baxter!" I called to him, through the bathroom door.

That brought him out from his ablutions fast enough.

"I hope you have your after-shave on," I told him. "You'll need to smell lovely for that one!"

"That's enough, Annie," he said.

"If you're nice enough, maybe she'll come and visit you in prison!" I said.

I was sorry the minute I said it.

He didn't even look angry, he just froze on me. Then he ran down the stairs towards her.

I went after him.

"You'll not want me around the place now you have company, Baxter," I said, still sour enough, for if he was upset over the police coming it was his own doing.

"I'll settle with you later," he said.

I cleared off, but not far.

He took her into the front room.

I could just about see them through the bushes.

They were on the sofa, but they weren't canoodling or carrying on. They were talking nineteen to the dozen. She gave him her white shoulder-bag to look in, and then he went out and up to his own room and then he came down again. She got up and he put his arm round her and said something, but it wasn't very lovey-dovey from the look on her face when she came out.

He walked her out to her car, and they had a long conversation, with her in the driving seat and Baxter talking through the rolled down window. Then she went off, without her white bag. No doubt Baxter would keep it and have a good excuse to go calling on her at the house instead of the hotel.

Baxter went back to the kitchen.

"Well?" I said, standing in the doorway.

"Well, what?" he said.

"Are you going to tell me what the police are after you for this time?" I said.

He called me a name.

"It's not you I'm fussed about!" I said. "It's Dad! Who is going to tell Dad?"

"The police weren't here after me at all, Annie," he said.

"Oh no," I said. "Of course not. Pull the other leg, it has bells on!"

He called me another name, that was worse than the first.

I just ran off. He had no call to use names like that, speaking about me. It wasn't me the police were round calling after, every other day.

I went down to the jetty, and sat there, with my feet in the water and my shoes on my knee. I could have wished that my Dad would come walking down the path to me and he'd give a shout and say my Mum was looking for me, but he didn't because he wasn't there, and my Mum wasn't there either, and we were all going to pieces, the whole family.

My mum would have known what to do about Baxter, to stop him getting himself into trouble with the police, and maybe landing up in jail.

But my Mum wasn't there any more, and my Dad was just a washout since she died, and there was only me left to cope.

I sat and looked at my shadow in the water, trying to think of things I could say to my Dad, and to Baxter, to try to make things better.

My old shadow on the water didn't say a word back to me.

I ended up just looking at myself.

I've thick, straightish hair, and that looked fine, but my old cardigan was baggy about me and, even allowing for the water wrinkles, my knees looked like the knees on a footballer.

I bet old Allie Sharry has knees like a gazelle.

5

I waited two hours nearly, not knowing what to do, and then I heard the Squirt. He was coming down the lane, all happy, with his new rod in his hand.

I went to meet him.

"What's wrong?" he said. He had only to look at me to know something was up.

I told him about the police, and Baxter.

"Holy smoke!" he said.

"So if you know anything, Peter, now is the time to tell me what it is," I said.

The Squirt looked uncomfortable.

"You *do* know something," I said.

"I don't," he said. "I'm only guessing."

"Guessing what?" I said. We'd gone into the barn, and he had started sorting out his new tackle, automatically, not really thinking about it. A bit of me was sorry. The new rod and the gear that went with it meant a lot to him. He'd been saving and saving only he never had enough. He wouldn't have managed it but Baxter stumped up some money, and said Peter could pay him back later. Later, with Peter's finances, was likely to be very much later. He had a new reel on the rod, too, and reels and rods cost money.

He picked up the reel, and played with it, fingering the release.

"Well?" I said.

"I don't want to believe it is what I think it could be," he said. "That's why I don't want to tell you. Because once I've said it, it is sort of real, isn't it? And if I'm wrong, I've still thought it, and made you think it too."

"You think Baxter has done something really bad," I said. "Worse than the bicycles?"

"He *says* he didn't do the bicycles," Peter broke in, "but supposing Baxter knew all along that they were stolen? You know what that makes him, don't you?"

I didn't want to say it. I didn't want it to be true. Everybody knew it was Marky Taylor, not Baxter, because Baxter isn't like that.

"Not Baxter," I said.

"Yeah, well, I hope not," said Peter. "Only . . . only . . ." He stopped, and then he chucked the new reel down on top of the plank table. "How about that?" he said.

"You bought that," I said. "And the rod."

"With Baxter's money," he said.

"You had *some* money," I said.

"Not enough. I never had enough. Baxter gave it me, most of it. There's nearly twenty quids' worth there. He said it was for me, to make up for me having a bad time."

"What bad time?" I said.

"You and Dad and all, getting at me, about

my hair and things," Peter said. "Going on and on and on. He said it was for that, and things not being the same around here since Mum died, and nobody having any money. He said I was to have some money for a change, and he gave me it. Nearly twenty quid . . . nearly twenty quid, Annie."

Twenty quid might not be a lot to some people, but down Cow Lane, it's riches. Baxter doesn't make that much in a week at the hotel and he gives in all his dole money to the house. I know that.

"Where did it come from, Annie?" Peter said. "Where did he get it?"

"I don't know," I said.

"I don't know either," said Peter.

We stood there looking at each other.

"Baxter and Marky Taylor," I said, bitterly.

"Exactly," he said.

"He *knows* Marky Taylor," I said. "Baxter knows the sort of thing Marky gets mixed up in, after the bicycles. He knows to stay away from him."

"And he isn't staying away, is he?" said Peter. "Despite all Dad said. He's in something with Marky, and the thing is . . . is it Marky, Annie, or is it him? Suppose he did know about the bicycles, all along? If he was lying about that . . ."

"He wasn't," I said. "He doesn't tell lies, Baxter doesn't."

36

But I knew that I didn't *know* that. I just felt it.

"I don't think it is bicycles he's stealing this time," Peter said. "He wouldn't be caught the same way twice. I asked him where the money came from, and Baxter made some joke about it. I didn't go on about it because . . . well, I was glad to get the money, wasn't I? It meant I could buy my gear."

"And now you've spent it, you're beginning to have a conscience," I said.

It was the wrong thing to say. Peter was really hurt. He went towards the door, away from me.

"Squirt?" I said. "Squirt, I didn't mean it."

"Yeah. Sounds like it," he said.

"We've got to stick together, Squirt," I said.

"Don't call me Squirt," he said. "I'm sick of that name."

"All right. *Peter.* Peter, we've got to stick together, to sort this out. You and me. Because if Dad hears about it first of all he'll kill Baxter, and then he'll . . . I don't know what he would do. It would just about finish him, I suppose, after Mum and everything."

"Well, what do we do, then?" he said.

I thought about it. "We think he's pinching things, right?" I said. "We think he's in it with Marky. It can't be just money from the bar, because if it was he wouldn't need Marky, so it must be *things.*"

"And the things must be somewhere," Peter said. "That's what I thought we'd find, when we went round the island. Some sort of hidey-hole, but there wasn't. And there's nothing hidden round the house, because I've looked and looked . . ."

"Not our house," I said. "What about the Taylors'?"

Peter shrugged.

"It would help if we knew what sort of things we were looking for," he said.

Something clicked in my mind.

"The bungalows!" I said. "The Major's tourist bungalows. The people up there have been missing things. I heard some of them on about it at Kominskis'."

"Neat!" said Peter. "Right on our front doorstep."

Oh Hell! I thought. *Then it must be true!*

"We'll have to face them with it," Peter said.

"Not till we can prove it," I said, because I knew that if Baxter was like we thought he was, then he would just deny it, and we would be no further on. He would go on and on stealing, and eventually the police would catch up with him and he and Marky would be put in prison.

"How do we prove it?" he said.

"We have to find some of the stolen stuff," I said. "They must have it somewhere, and we're more likely to find it than anybody else because we both live here, and we know where things might be hidden, and we *know* who is hiding them, not like the police, who just think it might

38

be Baxter and Marky." I was busy remembering the policemen nipping out of the car and searching round our barn and the bushes, while Sergeant Joe McDowell had Baxter in the house. That was very clever of them, and a very sneaky thing for Sergeant Joe to do.

"If we find the stuff, we can challenge Baxter with it, and tell him we'll go to the police if he doesn't stop stealing," I said.

"If he is stealing," Peter said.

"If he is," I said.

It felt like a betrayal.

6

"Annie Orr?" Marky Taylor said.

He'd popped up out of the bushes and ambushed me, in Stage One of the Save Baxter From Himself campaign.

I was supposed to be having a quiet look round Taylors', the sheds and things, and their old wonky work-hut, in case the tourists' things were hidden there.

"That's me," I said. "And that's our engine on your boat, Marky Taylor!" My idea was to switch over to the attack and start asking him things about our engine before he could ask me what I was doing on their land.

We'd agreed it would be me who tried round Taylors', while Peter searched our place more carefully, because if Peter got caught down there he was likely to get his head knocked off, and I would get away with a row if I was caught. Well, now I was caught.

"How come our engine is on your boat?" I said, keeping up the attack.

"Baxter," he said.

"Baxter doesn't own our engine," I said. "It isn't his to lend."

That was true, anyway. It was Baxter who

wanted the engine, but my Dad agreed to pay half. It didn't really belong to us even then, for neither of them had the money. They had to get it off Miles Sharry. He sold them the engine, and he docked it from my Dad's pay, only he charged so much that my Dad says we'll be paying it forever. The engine is like everything we have, it really belongs to the Sharrys, and is on a kind of a loan to us. Even the boat isn't ours. It went with the let of the house when Miles was doing the tourists, and he allowed us to have the use of it so my Dad can go down the lake, when the cruisers get in trouble. My Dad reckons he'd have had to have an engine for that anyway, but that didn't stop Miles Sharry from making us pay for it.

Marky hopped over their wall and swaggered over the grass towards me, chewing at a long stalk like John Wayne.

"You are like an old cow, Marky," I told him, backing off at the same time, because truth to tell I am a bit afraid of him. I wished I had had Peter with me.

"How so?" he said.

"Eating grass," I said. "You could die of that."

"Cows don't," said Marky.

"They're ruminants," I said, searching in my mind for a safe I've-said-nothing way to turn the conversation round to tourists losing things from their bungalows. I didn't want to ask him straight out if he was in the pinching with

Baxter, because I knew he would deny it, and I didn't know what else he might do.

"Rumin-*whats*?" he said.

"Rumin-something," I said, not too sure that I had remembered it right. "Grass eaters, Rumin-somethings."

He didn't look impressed, and I was running out of words.

"I like cows," I kind of gabbled at him, retreating all the time towards the path, and getting ready to make a run for it.

"You would!" said Marky scornfully. "You don't know anything about cows. Ever been to an abattoir? Walking Wimpys, that's cows! Specially if you add a slice of onion and a curly bap."

"I could easy get mad at you, Marky," I said.

"Well, don't," he said. "I am bigger than you are, Annie, and I don't fight fair."

It wasn't as bad as it might sound. He was grinning all over his scabby face. He would never raise a hand to me, or Baxter would cut it off for him.

"Big talker," I said, making it onto the path, and not before time.

"Oh now," he said. "See you? What age are you, Annie Orr?"

"Thirteen," I said. "You know I'm thirteen."

"Thirteen?" he said. "Well grow up a bit, Annie, and I'll take you places and show you things."

I didn't like the way he said it, not one bit. Any minute now and he'd be getting flirty, trying to stuff leaves down my neck or something like that. I can put up with back chat, but I couldn't put up with Marky in that mood.

"You're getting to be a nice wee chick, Annie Orr," he said. "Bumps in all the right places!"

That did it.

I wasn't standing round to have the likes of Marky Taylor make remarks about my figure. I headed for the hills, past the Taylors' old bungalow and up the lane towards our place, praying one of the cows would take a bite out of him. One of Marky's big sticky-out ears would do a cow's supper nicely.

Peter was waiting for me at our house. I didn't tell him what Marky said, because I didn't like to. It's embarrassing, a thing like that.

"Any luck?" Peter said.

I shook my head.

"What do we do now?" he said.

"There's one more place I know of," I said. "It's a kind of hidey-hole our Baxter has. I followed him there, one time, just to see where he was going."

"I'm not the only snoopy one in the family, then," Peter said.

I wasn't pleased. I'm not snoopy, it is just survival round here, where no one tells anyone else a thing. You have to find out for yourself.

No one told me that my Mum was ill, until it

was there for all to see, and then I had to know it. By then it was too late, for there was no time to do all the things I could have done for her to make it easy. All I could do was to make up my mind that I would look after my Dad and Baxter and Peter, so that no one could ever take them away from me without telling.

Looking after Baxter was what I was doing, not snooping.

7

We couldn't just go to Baxter's hidey-hole, it was more difficult than that.

The problem was the Taylors, and in particular Marky.

Baxter's hidey-hole is the Major's old boat-shed, tucked away in the reeds and trees at the mouth of the Broadfoot, which runs just behind the Major's bungalows. To get to it, you have to take my Dad's path out to the Point, and then duck onto the dog-path down amongst the reeds. When the dog-path peters out, you take to the mud. I reckon it was the mud that made Baxter pick it as a safe place to hide out, when he wanted to be on his own, and I thought that it was the most likely place for hiding things if he was stealing from the bungalows because it was right beside them, but hidden.

It was the place to look then, but to look there I had to cross the Taylors' land, and Marky might be lurking behind any old tree. He'd either nab me or start trying to chat me up, and I didn't know which would be worse.

"So the big plan is that I go *by boat*!" I told Peter.

"Stop!" he said. "Why don't I go?"

"You don't go, because you wouldn't be going there," I said. "You know there's no fish there, and Marky knows it, and Baxter knows it. But I don't go fishing, do I? So if I *did*, I might go somewhere no sensible fisherman would go, mightn't I? Like the mouth of the Broadfoot. And anybody seeing me would think I was just an idiot, and didn't know about the out-flow."

There is a farm outflow away up the Broad-foot. The fisherman are always on about it. The stuff comes down the Broadfoot and kills the fish.

"If you go by boat and Marky is on the look-out he is bound to see you," Peter objected.

"That's where you come in," I said. "If he sees me making for the Broadfoot, and he goes to head me off, he has to cross the mud, doesn't he?"

"Yes," said Peter, doubtfully.

"And you've just got new fishing gear, to have a go at the old pike out by Runey, right?" I said. "Everybody knows you are mad about it. So there you are out by Runey with your new gear, innocent as pie. And if Marky is about you can warn me."

"But I'll be too far way to do anything about it!" he said.

"No, you won't," I said. "Because you'll be wearing your mucky denim jacket, won't you? And beneath your denim jacket you'll have a red shirt on. Red for danger, see? If you take your jacket off, that means Marky is on his way over

46

the mud, and I've to row like mad in the opposite direction."

That's the way we did it.

Peter picked his stuff up and headed out for Runey and the reeds. I gave him time to get to the pike ground, and get set up on the bank, and then I started off in our boat, with his old rod rigged up the back. I pulled across the bay, past the Taylors' mouldy house with the tin roof, and then I started fishing by-the-way, but in fact I was letting her drift in towards the Broadfoot. I kept an eye on Peter, across the lake, waiting for the flash of red, and when it didn't come I let the boat drift in, closer and closer to the Broadfoot.

The Broadfoot is dark and narrow, despite the name. The Major used to have the boathouse on it, before he got into the bungalow business. Then he built a new boathouse on the other side, away from the outflow, and jetties for the visitors' boats. There is a boat for each bungalow and you get all class of people going there, but the Major doesn't tell them about the outflow running down the back, and killing off the fish, because a thing like that isn't good for business.

The old boathouse just lies there, derelict and forgotten about. For a while one year Baxter helped the Major out with his boats and the visitors, but then he had some class of a row with the Major, and the next year the Major didn't take him on. That would be when Baxter got to know about the boathouse being there. I

47

wouldn't have known about it at all, if it hadn't been for Baxter sneaking off there to be on his own.

It isn't much of a boathouse any more. Just tin sides, broken windows and a tin roof, and an open front letting down to a reed channel, just off the Broadfoot, with four piers inside. The Major had a wooden footbridge laid across to the boat-house from his side, but it collapsed long since, and the reeds are all over where it used to be, so there is no way in but by boat or by boots, through the mud.

I worked my way in through the reeds, till I had the boat square onto one of the piers. It was the most worrying bit, because I couldn't see Peter any more, and I'd no Marky-Taylor-is-coming alarm system. To balance that, no one could see me either. The reeds are like a forest there, especially if you are low down in a boat.

I got out onto the pier. It was all slimy, and green, some sort of algae from the outflow.

I took a step or two, and something scuttled, under the supports. That pulled me up short.

Must have been a rat!

It is no good being finicky about rats if you are going to spend your time round old boathouses. Just the same I went back to the boat and took the Priest from it. If you don't know what a Priest is you don't know about fishing, or boats. A Priest is what you send the fish to heaven with. In our boat it is the top of an old walking stick, loaded with a bit of lead. It copes fine with fish, and I had no doubt it would cope with a rat, if one jumped me. I knew that no rat would, but I didn't know whether the rats knew.

No rat came at me.

I hopped from one greasy pier to the next, and then ducked in beneath the cover, into the dark.

It wasn't totally dark, just half light, for the reeds had grown up round the windows outside, but it felt dark, because I'd just come from the bright sun outside. It took me a minute or two to get my eyes accustomed to the change, and then I started searching.

It was mucky.

There was an old stripey green mattress, that I just couldn't touch, because it was damp and oozey, with horse hair sticking out of it. Then there was a fridge somebody had dumped, and an old kitchen unit with the drawers hanging open. There was a German newspaper in one of the drawers, nothing else. The Major must have carted the unit out of one of the bungalows and stuck it in the boathouse.

Then there were the tyres. Round our lake people use them for building jetties. You mix them in with the concrete. It is a neat way of doing things, but the Major had a big pile left over, mouldering.

Tyres are terribly difficult to shift, and worse still when there's weed and old tin cans and whatnot mixed around them. You wouldn't believe some of the pale creepy crawlies that came hopping out to get me, waggling their feelers in the air. I don't go for creepy crawlies, and in the end I gave up. From the look of the wildlife that came out of the tyres they hadn't been moved for ages, anyway.

Then I tried the fridge.

The door was stuck tight. A fridge shouldn't have been left there, for no fridge should ever be put where some child or animal might hide in it. That is what Miss McCann told us after some little child in England got caught in one and nearly died. Her dog barked at the fridge, and they got her out. The English child was dead lucky . . . well, live lucky really, for she would have been dead if it hadn't been for her dog.

I was about five minutes trying to force the fridge door open, and then I did what I should have done in the first place and looked round the back.

There was no back to it, and nothing else inside either! Somebody had ripped the whole shooting works out.

I sat down on a tyre and told myself off.

Then I saw the screws.

New screws.

At first I didn't take in what a box of new screws would be doing sitting on a shelf in the old boathouse, but then I did.

I wish I hadn't.

No, I don't. I wouldn't like to think that I would miss a thing like that.

It was typical of Baxter. He should have hidden the screws when he had finished what he was doing with them, but he hadn't. If the policemen from Sergeant Joe McDowell's car had come snooping there the way they did in our shed I bet they would have spotted the screws in a minute, and worked out what they meant.

I followed the argument that if there were new screws sitting in a box in the old boathouse, then there had been some carpentry going on!

It didn't take me long to find it.

There was a cut in the board at the bottom of the old unit, smeared with mud so that no one could see. Two cuts in the plank, about a metre apart, and six bright new screw heads.

No screwdriver!

I went back to the boat and got our fishknife, then I ducked back under the cover and set to work. Another time I might not have managed it, but my blood was up! I put the knife blade in the screw notch, and hit it a ding with the lead headed Priest, the way I've seen my Dad do with his claw hammer. It didn't do much for the knife handle, but it lodged the blade, and then I started twisting.

Five screws I got out easily enough, but the sixth wouldn't budge. That's the story of my life.

I wasn't having that. It was decision time. I took hold of the knife and I forced her down between the planks and then I bang-banged on the handle, but it was no go. Then I lost my temper and I took the Priest and swiped at the unit and the plank split down the middle.

Victory!

A bit of jiggling got the broken plank out of the hole, and I was able to see in.

There was a bit of old blanket folded up inside. I folded it back.

A camera. A set of wire jump leads, and some boxes with electrical things in them, I hadn't a clue what they were. A pair of binoculars and a small white radio set, with the aerial bent.

Stolen from the Major's bungalows and carefully hidden in Baxter's hidey-hole.

Our Baxter *was* a thief.

8

I got our sack from the boat and put the stolen things in it, and then I beetled off out of there as fast as I could go.

I was all upset, poling out of the Broadwater reeds onto the sunlit lake, with a sackful of Baxter's guilty secrets at my feet.

A thief, but not caught *yet*.

Head for home, and confront him! That was my thought.

Then I saw the flash of red, way out amongst the reeds off Runey.

The warning signal!

Somebody must be out and about at Taylors', and the Squirt was warning me.

Row for home?

That was just what Marky would expect me to do, and he'd be lying in wait to ambush me. I'm clever enough not to run into a trap like that.

I rowed the *other* way, towards Bellaghery, and when I was rowing I had my Big Idea.

Marky and Baxter had been stealing things from the visitors in the Major's bungalows. I knew it, but I couldn't prove it. I could face Baxter with the stuff, and still he might deny it. Then there I would be with a pile of stolen stuff.

If I was caught with it, I might even get the blame myself!

My Big Idea was very simple.

If I could get the stuff back to the people it had been stolen from, all the fuss would stop!

It wasn't a bad idea, but there was one snag. How?

The Major has six bungalows. How could I know which thing had come from which bungalow?

That was when I had my second Big Idea, Plan Two.

Plan Two was to dump the stolen stuff in the sack on the Major's doorstep, and let him sort it out. Maybe he would think that it was the fairies!

Fairies or no . . . and the Major wasn't the Tinkerbell type . . . Once the stuff was recovered nobody would be that bothered. It would be found well away from Baxter's hidey-hole and nobody would be able to say it had had anything to do with him, or Marky Taylor. The police might think that it was them, but they couldn't prove it *and* I'd be able to tell Baxter what I had done, and give him such a scare at nearly being caught that he would stop his thieving! I'd be able to tell him that if I could find the stolen things as easily as I had, then the police would have had no bother at all, once they put their minds to it.

It seemed a good plan. The more I thought

about it, it seemed the only plan that would save us. I just couldn't stand the idea of the ructions there would be if my Dad ever found out. My Dad has grown such a lonely old thing, walking round the lake on his own, and not even asking me to go with him, when I would if I was asked. Since my Mum went he has no one of his own. I found some letters down the side of the chair. They were from a marriage bureau. It was called the Happy Club. I couldn't even say to him about them, because I couldn't find the words. I was there to look after him, he didn't need some old widow woman.

I was there to look after him, and if saving him meant getting rid of Baxter's stolen things before he was caught, then I was the one to do it!

As I thought, I kept moving. I pulled the boat in towards the jetty behind the Major's. All I had to do was nip into his yard and dump the stuff, and get away off out before I was collared.

The big bet in Plan Two was that the Major wouldn't be there, only Cromwell. Cromwell is the Major's dog. Cromwell is a nice old thing. I would have no trouble with Cromwell. He would give me a lick and send me on my way and when the police came and asked who dumped the sackful of stolen things on the Major's doorstep old Cromwell wouldn't bark a dicky-bird!

I wasn't worried about the big bet, because the Major goes off to Sharry's Hotel at a quarter to one every day, and he is there all afternoon in the Lounge Bar. It keeps him out of the reach of the people in his bungalows. As I drifted in it was almost half one, so I was on a safe thing.

I rehearsed it in my mind to see that I had Plan Two right. Nip out of the boat, round the side of the house, into the Major's yard, say hello Cromwell, dump my bag with the evidence in it, back to the boat and off. Then I would have to go like the clappers to get up to Bellaghery Continental Restaurant in time to do my bit for the Black Economy! Getting to Kominskis' was the only real problem I would have, especially if Marky Taylor was lying in wait at our jetty!

I got out of the boat, sack in hand, and made my way through the bushes. I'd come in at the Major's own jetty, not the one he uses for the visitors' boats. He has his own boat there, the catamaran. I was able to edge in beside her without bumping, and tie our boat onto the gooseberry hedge, which was great apart from the prickles!

The hedges are thick around the Major's house and that was to my advantage. I reckoned that I would be on the lookout and any of the Major's visitors who happened to be about would not be, so I could keep out of sight if any of them saw me . . . that is, they *wouldn't* see me, because I would stay hunkered in the hedges till they went past with their swimming flippers or rods or whatever they were planning to leave around their bungalows next time to tempt people into stealing.

There were no visitors.

The only single solitary soul about the place was Cromwell. He was out on the drain cover, sunning himself. He lifted his head and gave me a tail wag as I went past, and I gave him the time of day and went round the side of the house and right up to the Major's back door, sack in my hand.

I didn't *sneak* round. I just marched up, on the off chance that if anybody did see me I would look respectable, whereas if I was caught sneaking with a sack filled with stolen things it wouldn't be Baxter who was carted off to prison and put my Dad round the bend, it would be me. Not that Baxter would let that happen. He would own up, but getting Baxter into the hands of the police was the last thing I wanted.

In round the back to the Major's, past his shed, up to the back door.

Then . . .

PANIC!

The Major was at his window, looking out at me from his big red chair.

He waved me in!

I stopped dead, caught in the act.

The Major had on his green shirt with the sleeves rolled up. He has a red and rusty face, red hair that grows in tufts, what there is of it, and, as usual, he had a glass in his hand.

He was all pleased to see me!

"Young Miss Orr!" he boomed at me. "To what do I owe the pleasure?" He came bounding out of his chair, and bounced through the door.

"You're here, Major," I said, which wasn't very bright of me, though I wasn't likely to do an Einstein in the circumstances.

"Indeed I am," he said. "Come in for a dram."

"I . . . I don't drink, Major," I said.

"Of course you don't!" he boomed. "Too young. But I dare say I can fix something for your pleasure that your good mother won't object to!"

He shouldn't have said it. I have no mother now. He knows that. Maybe he just forgot.

"I'm in a hurry, Major," I said, clutching at my sack, and wondering if he could make out the shapes that were inside it. In a minute he would demand that I showed him what I'd got there, and then I would either be arrested or I'd have to take to my heels and run off, and the fat would be in the fire because he would guess what I'd been at and have the police after me.

"In a hurry!" he said. "And what brings you in a hurry down here?"

I just gaped at him. What could I say? Why should I be caught so far out of my way, with a big sack?

"Come on, child. I won't bite you!" he boomed, cheerfully.

"Turnips!" I said.

It was the first thing that came into my head. There was a big pile of rotted turnips over by the fence, sitting looking at me, and they were the first thing I saw, so I said it, just like that: "Turnips, Major!"

"Turnips?" he said.

"I'm ... I'm ... I'm working with the Kominskis, now," I said, beginning to get on top of my lie. "I have a job in the kitchen helping Petra. And they're needing turnips, and they haven't got any and I said you grew some and maybe you could let us have one ... one or two ..."

I was quite pleased with myself. A Natural Born Liar, and I'd proved it!

Then my heart gave a jump. Suppose he gave me the turnips? Then he'd say: "Where's your money to pay for them?" and I was out with no money for it was all at home in the Housekeeping Box on the dresser. I'd have to say "I have no money with me, Major, for I forgot it," and then he would drop into Kominskis' and ask about his turnip money and I would be completely caught out.

"There are no turnips here, child!" he boomed at me. "What there was, is rotten in the ground, since the lake rising!"

"Oh!" I said, hopping off the hook, "oh dear! Well, I'm sorry I bothered you, Major. I'll have to go off to Sharry's shop then."

"You'll find that all Mr Sharry's establishments are shut!" he said.

"Shut?" I said.

If the hotel was shut, that accounted for the Major not being down in the bar talking about his experiences in Burma. By *why* shut?

" 'Closed Due to Unforeseen Circumstances, Eileen Sharry' says the notice on the door. Shop, hotel and the whole shooting works!"

"Oh," I said.

"No Room at the Inn!" he boomed. "A Pub with No Beer! And that is a serious unforeseen circumstance to a man in my position!"

"Well then, I'll have to tell the Kominskis they're not getting their turnips!" I said.

No turnips it was. I went off with my sack, congratulating myself on getting out of one problem, but at the same time landing myself with another.

The boat.

I couldn't march back to the boat, because the Major would wonder why I'd come all the way to his house to collect turnips in a boat, when I could have walked down from the Kominskis quicker! And I couldn't leave the boat where it was and head off on foot, because sooner or later the Major would go for a stroll and spot it, and then there'd be all sorts of questions needing answers.

What I did was to walk away from the house, up past Cromwell's old panty tongue where he was sunning himself, and then dodge into the bushes, and creep-creep-creep back expecting the Major to come out and stop me any minute.

He didn't.

I got to the boat, and cast off as quick as I could.

It took me too much time.

I was already late for the Kominskis' when I got back to the boat, and then I had to row like mad to get back to our house, hoping and praying I wouldn't have a Marky Taylor problem to contend with when I got to the jetty.

No Marky, and no sign of the Pike Fisherman with the red danger signal shirt on the distant bank of Runey either!

I needed Peter, but I couldn't afford to wait about for him to turn up. I needed him, because I had the sack still and I had to do something with it. I couldn't just leave it lying around in my room for somebody to find.

My first thought was to dump the sack in the lake, with a plastic float on top, so that I could row round later and hook it out. Then I thought that that would be almost a second stealing for if the camera and stuff were worth anything, then a dip in the water might well steal the value away. My second thought was to do a Jackie Daw and seal it up somewhere in a hiding place . . . but I couldn't risk that, in case the police came back for another search round our house. I was pretty well convinced that anywhere I could hide it would be somewhere they could find it, if they looked hard enough.

I did the only other thing I could think of, in my hurry.

I took it with me.

I was counting on being able to hide it somewhere up Cow Lane, well away from our house. I thought I could drop it in the hedge where it would be waiting for me to pick up on my way back, when I would have time to think of a proper hiding place for it.

Great Thinking.

All problems solved, so long as some dishonest person didn't come along, say: "There's a sack that looks full of something", open it up, and make off with the contents.

That wasn't much of an idea. Getting the things back to the people that owned them in the first place was the centre of my plan, and having some tinker walk off with them was no way to set about it.

I was still in two minds (or no mind at all) about what to do with my sack when I got to the top of Cow Lane and turned to walk down to the Kominskis', but what I found waiting for me then decided it.

There were two police landrovers blocking the road, one on each side, so that cars going past had to zig-zag between them, and there must have been half a dozen policemen, all dolled up in their flak jackets.

A road block for the IRA, and I had to walk straight into it!

I'm a braver person than I thought I was.

I took a grip on my sack and walked towards the policemen, casual as you please.

"Hi there, Annie Orr!" said Trevor Cromie. "How is your Da keeping this weather?"

"Keeping well," I said, and I was past him. He was up on the ditch with a sub machine gun hanging round his neck, and his hand gun unbuttoned in his holster. All the policemen have guns round here, because of the terrorists. Normally the sight of a policeman with a gun wouldn't worry me, but this time I had the feeling that their machine guns were pointing at me. I was half expecting a rat-tat-tat of bullets in my back.

I'd never trust the like of Trevor Cromie with a gun, if it was me. We went to the same primary school, only he was just going out of it when I was coming in. He used to write up rude things about the teachers.

I could hear the radios chattering away in the back of the landrovers, and one of the policemen gave me a wink when I went past him, but I never even smiled at him once.

Nobody stopped me. Nobody looked in my sack. Nobody paid me a bit of attention.

I didn't look back all the way down to

Kominskis', and it never crossed my mind to wonder why the police had picked that day for blocking the Bellaghery Road, out of all the days in the year.

That just goes to show how mixed up I was.

9

Petra was standing at the door when I got there.

"Hi, Anna, what time is this?" she asked me.

Nobody else calls me Anna. My name is Annie. Petra always does. She says Anna is a nice name and I am a nice person and why shouldn't I have it. It is all the same to me.

"Sorry," I said. "I got held up."

"The world is held up today!" she said, nodding up the road towards the police landrovers. "Police!"

I don't think Petra is very keen on the police. She never *exactly* says what happened to them before they left Hungary, but I don't think it can have been good. I've seen the old TV newsreels about the Hungarian Revolution. I expect Petra and Lazlo were out in the streets chucking things at tanks like the rest of them. Anyway, they never speak about going back to Hungary. It is a bit of their life they keep to themselves. Maybe they do speak about it, but if they do it is in Hungarian. They speak to each other in Hungarian when they don't want the customers to know what they are saying.

"What have you here?" Lazlo said, looking at my sack. "The groceries?"

Instinctively I switched the sack to the other hand, away from him. "Some things for the house," I said.

"Shopping in Cow Lane?" Petra said, raising an eyebrow at me. She has a sort of flexi face, with eyebrows that jump about. It isn't pretty, but it is a nice face, except when you do some horrible crime like letting the cream boil when she's in the middle of her Magyar Surprise or something like that. Then she looks you dead in the eye and tells you what you should have done with it, and then she turns round to Lazlo and she tells him in Hungarian what she'd like to do to you. At least, I think that that is what she tells him.

She's nice.

They're both nice, actually, but I could have wished they wouldn't start one of their comedy numbers about my sack.

"Cow Lane General Stores!" said Lazlo, his brown eyes glittering at me.

"Mushrooms?" said Petra, suddenly.

"There are no mushrooms down by us," I said.

I was dead clever.

You only have to tell the Kominskis there isn't something or something can't be done for them to start telling you where it can be found or how to do it, and when the 'it' is food they argue about it as well.

The attention switched from my sack to mush-

66

rooms. Apparently there are *great* mushrooms round here, but Lazlo wasn't telling me where. Then Petra started her bit about rice and mushrooms in beer batter and they were off.

I took the sack to the hall, and carefully hung it up with my anorak. The sack first, and then the anorak on top, in case anybody accidentally knocked it off. I don't think Lazlo or Petra would look inside. They are decent people, not nosey like me.

I came back into the action rolling the sleeves of my jersey up.

"Here I am," I said. "Better late than never. What am I doing today?"

"You serve all the customers!" said Petra, over her shoulder. She was standing blocking the door. Lazlo had gone outside again, and was sitting on their bench. I could hear him, but I couldn't see him. He was keeping up a running commentary about what was going on at the road block.

"What customers?" I said.

"Any customers that come," said Petra. "We are the bosses and we are on strike. You do the work."

"What about the kitchen?" I said. "Shouldn't I be getting things ready for tonight?"

Outside, Lazlo said something which sounded very rude, in Hungarian. Petra laughed, and then she said to me: "Lazlo says there will be no customers, with the police shouting at everyone.

67

And he is right! If there are customers we serve a reduced menu; Rhubarb Soup, Bellaghery Goulash or Tokaj Pork Chops, followed by Floating Islands. All of that we have ready. While the siege goes on, we strike! You can't strike, because you are the workers! So you serve the customers their tea and buns!"

Kominskis' isn't really a restaurant. Not like other restaurants anyway. It is the front room of their house. It has an old farmhouse fire, and a low ceiling with bare beams, and a staircase leading out of it to upstairs where they live. They do most of their business at night when they serve proper Hungarian meals, but during the day they are open from ten o'clock and they do cups of coffee and special things that Petra makes up. She does Gooseberry Strudel, Wasps' Nests (they're all sugary, butter and yeast with a hot vanilla sauce added after), Sponge Kisses (which are great nibbles) and Honey Pogácsas. Her Wasps' Nests are delicious, and she's started on showing me how to bake them, so one day I can surprise everyone. Lazlo does the dishes and the vegetable growing out their back, and helps a bit with the cooking, but it is Petra who is the real genius.

"I'll just stand here, then?" I said, feeling awkward about it, for I was being paid after all, and I thought I ought to be doing something.

"If you complain, Anna, I sack you!" Petra said, and she gave me one of her bouncy grins.

I've never seen a face bounce like that, but hers does. It must be something about being Hungarian.

"And don't eat all the buns!" Lazlo's voice echoed back from outside.

In the end I went out and sat with them in the sun. Lazlo was on the seat, and Petra had curled up her legs on the step, and we all watched the policemen.

They were stopping the cars coming *out* of Bellaghery, but they just waved through the cars going in.

They started talking to each other in Hungarian, and every so often Petra would give me a translation when she thought I was feeling left out of things.

"Half across Europe we've come, to get away from policemen and guns and roadblocks, and here we are again, with it all happening on our doorstep!" Petra told me.

"Just like home!" said Lazlo.

"Just one roadblock," I said. Roadblocks aren't unusual round here, because of the IRA.

"Not one!" said Lazlo. "Every road!"

"What?" said Petra.

"I told you. Every road in and out of Bellaghery, there is a block!" said Lazlo. "That is why we have no customers!"

"Why Bellaghery?" Petra asked.

"There must be something big on," I told her. Maybe they had had a tip off that one of the famous IRA men was coming through, or maybe they had turned up an Arms Dump.

"Perhaps one of the big English men in Government is coming?" Petra said.

They wittered on.

I'd lost interest in the roadblocks. I was back thinking about my sackful of guilty secrets, hanging innocently in their hallway.

Supposing the police came and searched? Wouldn't it be awful if the sack turned up in Kominskis', and everybody said they had stolen the things? Bang would go the Black Economy as far as Annie Orr was concerned.

They chattered on, and I worried on, going in every so often to check on my sack, to see that it was still where I'd left it . . . though who I thought was going to move it on me was a mystery!

Then we had customers.

Two of the policemen came in and sat down and had coffee and Wasps' Nests and Kossuth bread. They sat there with their big black guns on and talked about baseball, and then they went off again.

"Well?" Petra said, putting her head round the kitchen door. She had retreated from the front step when the policemen came.

"Well what?" I said.

"Did you hear what it was all about?"

"New York Yankees!" I told her.

Then two more came. The first two must have

told them about the Wasps' Nests. They didn't talk about much, they just ate, and then one of them smoked a cigarette, very slowly, and then they went off again. If they did say anything, they didn't say it while I was there listening . . . and I was accidentally within earshot in the kitchen most of the time!

I was heart scared about my sack. Suppose one of them knocked it off the hook, coming in the door? I should never have hung it there for all to see, full of stolen things.

I was glad to see the backs of the policemen, and was thinking about the end of my stint, when I had to face walking up the road past them, and through the police block and down our lane, and I thought it was more than I could bring myself to do!

I hung around, hoping the police would pack it up and go away, but they didn't.

"Are you not away home, Anna?" Petra asked me.

"I'll be off in a minute," I said.

"Nothing the matter, is there?" she said.

"No," I said.

I may have sounded a bit snappy, but I know what it was that made me sound that way. Another one wanting to mother me! Petra is always a bit that way. She thinks the Orrs can't look after themselves. She's always dropping hints by-the-way she could help out if there are any problems and is there anything I'm worried

71

about because if there is I'm to know I have her to turn to. Well, I do know, but what I had to worry about this time wasn't something I could discuss with some old stranger, even if she wasn't really a stranger, but just a good neighbour helping out.

There's more than Petra has dropped me hints about needing a helping hand, but I tell them I don't need one. I can look after myself, because I have to, *and* I can look after rest of the Orrs, for all I'm only thirteen years old. I was looking for a way out of the conversation when one came through the door, all tarted up in her tight white pants.

Allie Sharry again, Baxter's girlfriend, only Baxter wouldn't have been pleased to see her, for she was with a man.

I thought it would be her real boyfriend, but after a minute I decided it couldn't be, for he called her Miss Sharry.

They had some coffee, and a helping each of Petra's Strudel.

I stayed in the kitchen watching them. The tight pants and the long hair didn't seem to be working, for the man with her didn't look comfortable at all, despite the close up attention he was getting.

Allie Sharry was doing all the talking.

They got up to go, and then Allie asked could she go to the bathroom, and out she came by the back.

"I was hoping I'd catch you, Annie," she said.

Were you now? I felt like telling her, for it would be the first time she'd ever paid any attention to me.

"Would you give Baxter a message for me?" she said. "You're to tell him it is on for tonight."

"What is on?" I said.

"He'll know what I mean," she said, and she gave me a look.

"Don't you be leading our Baxter astray!" I told her.

"The cheek of you!" she said, by-the-way cheerfully, but there was something about her eyes that wouldn't wake up and be cheerful, just the same. I've never seen her with a face like that on her before.

She went back to her beau . . . and she never went near the bathroom.

I watched them down the road, with Lazlo on the bench beside me making remarks in Hungarian about her bottom. At least I think that was what he was on about, from the way Petra shut him up.

"That's the first time I've seen her in your place," I said.

Petra looked at Lazlo. Then she said, "It's all right, Anna, don't worry about it."

Worry about it? I didn't know what she was on about.

"The Sharrys *know* you work here," she said. "In case you were worrying that your Dad would get into trouble."

"Why would he get into trouble?" I said, and then I got it!

We are Sharry Slaves, more or less. Miles owns the house, and he thinks he owns the family, and Miles has it in for the Kominskis because they've taken some of his business. Maybe he wouldn't be too pleased to have one of *his* slaves working for the opposition!

"We're not afraid of Miles Sharry, if that is what you mean," I said.

"He's a good man,' Petra said.

I made a face.

"Did you know it was Miles suggested we get you to help us?" Petra said.

You could have knocked me down with a feather.

"He was worried about you," she said.

Old Miles? Worried about me? I could have told her a few stories about Miles! Maybe he reckoned I would wreck the restaurant, and all his customers would come back!

"You mustn't think everybody is against you, Anna," Lazlo said. "You've plenty of friends, if only you knew it."

The Kominskis don't *know*. That's because they are not from here. I could have told them Miles Sharry would do them no favours, nor me neither!

"You won't make friends, Anna, if you go round distrusting people. You'll end up like Jackie Daw," Petra said, gently.

Well, I have reason enough to distrust people. They all knew about my Mum, Petra included, and none of them told me, not even Dad. I have no reason to trust anybody around Bellaghery if I don't want to.

"Sometimes I wish people would just leave me alone," I said.

Petra's face fell, and for a moment I was sorry, but then I wasn't. They meant to be kindly, but I don't want people interfering in my life. I thought I'd better say something to switch the conversation, before I ended up having a row, and losing my job.

"That old Allie Sharry," I said. "She is leading our Baxter a dance!"

"Baxter?" said Petra.

"He fancies her like mad," I said. "But she doesn't fancy him!"

And then I had it, all in a second. If Baxter was stealing things for money, *she* was why he was doing it. He hasn't the money to go dating a college student like Allie Sharry. Maybe she was putting him up to it even, egging him on to buy her things.

"Green eyes!" Petra said, suddenly.

"What?" I said.

"Jealousy," she said.

I was taken aback by that, I can tell you, coming from Petra.

"Not good enough for your brother," said

Petra, "Is that it?"

"It is nothing to me who Baxter chooses to go out with!" I said, carefully. Now I'd realised it was Allie Sharry who was behind all the stealing, I knew I mustn't let on.

If I realised it, maybe they would.

Petra laughed. "A little mother!" she said.

I was mad at her. I think she knew it. She shouldn't have said a cruel thing like that to me.

"Anna?" she said.

"I think I'd better be going now, Mrs Kominski," I said, stiff as you please.

"Anna, wait a minute!" Petra said.

But I'd upped and grabbed the sack and my anorak and I was off up the road, policemen or no policemen.

By the time I hit Cow Lane I'd had myself arrested and sent to prison half a hundred times, but in reality nobody said a word to me. The police were too busy searching cars.

I went down the lane thinking about my mother, dead and buried up in the Presbyterian graveyard in Bellaghery, and how we were together once, and a family, but now we weren't any more. My Mum would have known what to do about poor Baxter and that Allie Sharry one, twisting him round her little finger and making him buy her things and take her places he couldn't afford.

I wasn't going to let her away with it. I was going to face up to Baxter and tell him Allie was fooling him, and he was betraying my Mum and my Dad and me and Peter and everyone with his lying and stealing.

That's what I was going to do.

10

I'd made up my mind to have it out with Baxter about his lying and his stealing and his college girlfriend putting him up to it, but *again* it didn't work out that way.

There was a car outside our house.

It wasn't a police car this time, but a little blue Mini with the sunlight winking on the roof, and a waggly pink dog on a bit of elastic dangling in the window, like a mad powderpuff.

Baxter was waiting at the door, posted there to intercept me, only I didn't know it.

"Hold on a minute, Annie," he said.

"Baxter . . ." I began.

"Annie?" My Dad's voice called from the kitchen.

I wasn't expecting my Dad to be there. He should have been at Sharry's Hotel. Then I remembered that it was all shut up.

"In you go, Annie, and mind your manners!" Baxter said.

I went in.

There was a woman in the kitchen, with my Dad.

"Annie," he said. "This is Margaret McVeigh. Margaret, this is Annie, the lady of the house!"

"Pleased to meet you, Annie," she said, holding her podgy hand out to me. She had a bracelet loaded with charms rattling round her wrist, and scarlet nails out of a paint pot.

I looked at my Dad. He gave me a smile, and put his hand on my shoulder.

"Annie?" he said.

I shook the woman's hand, without looking her in the eye. Peter was over against the wall. His face was pale, and his eyes were fixed down on the floor. He didn't look once at me either.

I didn't know what to make of it. What was she, some kind of housekeeper? She was small, and dumpy, with grey hair. There was a stiffness about her, as if she was on edge. She had furry boots, and she kept her knees clamped tight together as if they were welded that way. She was on the edge of the sofa, her back uncomfortably straight, as if she thought she'd catch something from the furniture.

The clothes basket was beside her. My Dad should have moved the clothes basket before letting her sit down. It was filled to overflowing with vests and socks and things.

My eyes went round the room. Lucky enough I had tidied things up before I went out, but only after a fashion. Peter's fishing bag was under a chair, and his rod was on the table. There were dishes on the draining board, and the broom cupboard was half open, and there were papers on the floor where somebody had spilled something.

"You have a nice home, Annie," the woman said.

"Yes," I said, "we like it," giving her back as good as I got. I could see what she was seeing. A house with everything every whichway, and Baxter with his frayed shirt, and Peter his mucky denim jacket and my Dad all done up like a dog's dinner.

"I'm glad I came down here with you, Dan," she said.

Dan!

Who was she to be calling *my* Dad 'Dan'?

"How about a cup of tea?" my Dad said, breaking the silence. He moved, and I moved at the same moment, making for the range.

He let me do it.

"Annie is our housekeeper, these days!" he told the woman.

"She's a great girl," the woman said.

I could feel their eyes on me, though I had my back to them.

I got out the mugs. I wasn't giving her the good china. I didn't give her anything to eat, either. I would have, but there wasn't a bun or a biscuit in the house.

The woman tried talking to me, but I wasn't having any of that. I'd made up my mind what she was after! I just got her her tea and then I said to my Dad that I had things to do.

80

"You'll excuse me, I'm sure," I said politely to the woman.

I went out.

My Dad came out into the yard after me.

"Annie?" he said.

"What's she here for?" I said.

"She's just a . . . friend of mine," he said.

"Oh yes?" I said, and I turned round on him. "Is that the best they could do for you?"

His face darkened over.

"They?" he said.

"I know all about it!" I told him. "I've seen the old letters they sent you, stuffed down the side of the chair!"

He turned on his heel and went back into the house.

"I do the housework round here!" I yelled at him. "If you want to keep things hidden from me then you shouldn't leave your old letters stuffed down the side of your chair for anyone to read!"

He didn't hear me.

I turned and I ran.

I wound up by the lakeside as usual, looking out over the water and wishing I could cut my tongue out. I didn't know how I could ever go back and face him.

He is *my* Dad, and he shouldn't have brought a woman like that to our house, not without telling me first so that I could have everything right.

81

He must have had a letter from his old Happy Club Marriage Bureau that I didn't see.

They'd send him a wee fat widow woman to keep him company.

It was only because he was lonely. I knew that, and worse than that was that I knew I'd hurt him, and showed him up in front of Mrs McVeigh.

Well, she wouldn't come back to Dan Orr's house in a hurry after the greeting I gave her, and it would be no loss, for I could have told him there are things you can't get out of a mail order book, or a 'Happy Club' which is much the same thing, only the goods come on two legs.

I was sorry for him, and in a way I was sorry for her, for she'd meant no harm only she shouldn't have landed unannounced on me, expecting a big hooray and the best china laid out.

But most of all I was sorry for myself, for I'd put my big foot in it and made a scene, and probably upset both of them, when they were doing no harm.

The sensible bit of me said that, and the other bit kept saying that no Mail Order Happy Club woman was going to barge in and try to take my Mum's place.

There was a step behind me, and I turned round.

It was my Dad.

"She's gone now, wee Annie," he said.

He put his arm round me, and gave me a hug.

"Have a good cry," he said. "It will take the bad feeling out of you."

We were there a while, down the jetty, but neither one of us said much.

It was good of him to send her off in her car and come down to me, when I was hurting.

We sat down by the jetty, talking.

He said a lot of things about my Mum, and missing her, and I told him I was missing her too.

"And I don't want . . . I don't want . . . " I tried to tell him, but he wouldn't let me.

"Shush, now, Annie," he said.

In the end he took me back up the house and he made me a cup of tea and we were really together, like we haven't been for months and neither of us said a word, any word about *Margaret*, or whatever her name was.

Then he told me he had to go off now, for he was needed down at Bellaghery.

"I thought the hotel was shut for the day?" I told him, not wanting him to go.

"Aye. It is," he said.

"What for?"

"There's no need to bother your head with that," he said. "You've had enough for one day!"

It was then I almost told him about the sack, but I couldn't. I just couldn't. I'd bust enough up for him.

"I've *got* to do," he said, awkwardly. "Otherwise I wouldn't. The Sharrys . . . "

"Rule our lives," I told him, "Like Kings and Queens."

"Kings and Queens have their troubles," he said.

I didn't know what he was getting at.

He stood there looking at me, with his face sombre, all in brown wrinkles. I could see Peter's face in him, though Peter's face is thinner; but Peter's face is clear, and his eyes are bright eyes, with life going on behind them. My Dad's eyes aren't like that any more. It is as if a part of him had shrivelled up inside. He was in his brown suit, the one with the baggy pockets. He must have put it on for her, the mail-order woman, but I doubt it she would have been impressed. His big, awkward hands came out the end of the sleeves like two grappling irons, and you could see the strength of his wrists, and the bulk of his shoulders; the strength was still there, don't get me wrong, but there was something missing inside him.

I felt like shaking him. For a minute there, talking to me as we hadn't talked for ages, he'd come alive, but now he was going funny on me again.

"I really must go now, Annie," he said, awkwardly. "It would be this day, of all days, with her coming and the whole world at sixes and sevens."

Then I knew what he was talking about. It wasn't the Sharrys at all. It was the Baxter thing. He'd heard talk of the police being down to our place to interview Baxter about the stealing.

He went off, and I was left all alone with my troubles, because the Sharrys needed their slave, even if they had taken it into their heads to shut up shop for the day.

He went because he had to, I know that now, but at the time I was so busy blaming the Sharrys for everything that I just couldn't see past it. All I could see was that it wasn't enough for them and their big money to rule our lives, they had to run them too.

I went back up to the house telling myself what I thought of the Sharrys and their dear sweet seventeen year old daughter in particular. Baxter was in the kitchen holding my sack.

"What's this, Annie?" he said.

11

I wasn't ready for it.

Like my Dad said, I'd had too much for one day.

"Well?" Baxter said, holding out the sack.

"You know," I said.

Baxter looked at me without blinking, only a puzzled expression came over his face. He was going to lie about it!

"I know?" he said.

"Sure you do. It is your stuff. You stole it, Baxter Orr, from the Major's bungalows."

"Eh?" he said.

He looked plain amazed. I'd been expecting him to shout at me and call me names or clout me one or something, but he did nothing like that. He looked at me as if he thought I'd gone mad.

"It was in your hidey-hole!" I told him. "Screwed up in a secret place behind the boards, where you thought no one would find it."

"Hold on, Annie!" he said, going red in the face. "Watch what you're saying. Either you are mad or I am mad, for I don't know what you are talking about."

"You stole it so you'd have lots of money to spend on her!" I said. "That Sharry one!"

He stood there gaping at me.

"Allie?" he said.

"You're a thief, Baxter Orr!" I said.

"I am not!" he said.

It doesn't sound much, but it was the way he said it. Suddenly the certainty of it began to drain out of me. Supposing he wasn't? Supposing it was all something Peter and I had just worked up between us?

"You're telling me you didn't steal those things?" I said.

"Steal what?" he said, exasperated.

"The things I found in your hidey-hole!" I said.

"No," he said, just straight and simple like that. Either he was the best actor in the world or . . .

"I don't believe you," I said, uncertainly.

Well, I didn't. Or I was almost certain I didn't.

"What do you mean, '*Stole*'?" he said. "And what's this about a hidey-hole? I haven't got a hidey-hole that I know of."

"You have, and that was in it!" I said. "In the bottom of the old rotten unit, hidden away beneath the boards. In the Major's boatshed where you go when you are fed up. And you are the only one round here that goes there. You know you are!"

"I know no such thing," said Baxter.

I knew he was telling me the truth. I've lived

87

around our house long enough to know when one of them is lying to me, or putting me off. Baxter was telling the truth.

"Somebody stole them!" I said. "Somebody hid them there. There are valuable things in that sack. Things that were taken from the Major's bungalows."

Maybe it was Marky Taylor all along, that was the thought that flashed in my head. Marky, and Baxter knew nothing about it.

Baxter up-ended the sack on the kitchen floor. The camera and all the other stuff fell out. He kicked at them with his foot.

"Junk!" he said.

"But . . . "

"Look at it!" he said. "Old and mouldy. God knows how long that stuff has been lying around. I don't steal things, Annie Orr, whatever else I may get up to that you don't approve of. I'm no thief! But if I was, I'd be sure to steal something that was worth stealing." There was an edge of anger coming in his voice, now that he'd figured out what I was saying about him.

"I'm no thief, Annie Orr," he repeated, and he barged out through the door, leaving me looking at the pile of things on the floor.

He was right.

They were old and mouldy.

Only an idiot would steal them and hide them away as if they were the crown jewels, like an old jackdaw.

A *Jackdaw*!

I was never so ashamed in my life. Me thinking it was Baxter looting the Major's bungalows, when all the time . . .

. . . old Jackie Daw. Old Jackie, not-right-in-the-head-Jackie and his collections of useless treasures from the rubbish bins that he hid from the Welfare woman.

The rakings of the bins!

And I'd been guarding them with my life, carting them up and down and all around the place, expecting the police to close in on me at any minute.

I went looking for Peter. He was having a moody in the barn.

"Oh, Squirt," I said. "We got it all wrong!" Then I had to tell him what I'd done; how I'd found the stuff and faced Baxter with it, and now Baxter was mad at me.

"You might have known from the look of the stuff!" Peter said, kicking the old radio with his foot. "Anyway, I could have saved you the trouble, if you'd asked me first . . . and it was supposed to be a *Joint* Operation, wasn't it?"

"I never had time," I said. "Any road, what do you mean, you could have saved me the trouble?"

"I'll show you," he said, and he took me round to the back of the woodpile.

"You remember I gave you the red signal, when you were out in the boat? Marky and

Baxter showed up in Sharry's old van. That's what I was signalling about. They came *here*."

"To our barn?" I said.

"Yep!" he said. "When they cleared off, I came back and took a closer look. And I found *this*."

"I don't see anything," I said.

"Neither did I, and neither did the coppers!" he said, with a grin.

"Neither did the coppers what?" I said.

"Watch this!" he said.

He bent down, and dug his fingers into the ground. The next minute, a whole big bit of the earth came way in his hand. It wasn't rough, it was a neat cut, like a sod, only there was no grass on it. He lifted another, and another and another. Each one of them was about fifteen centimetres thick and thirty centimetres square, and beneath them was a plank they'd been sitting on. He piled the sods up neatly behind him, and when he raised the last one, he raised the plank after it.

"Take a look!" he said.

I squatted down, and looked in the hole. It was very neat, with wooden sides, like a buried box, only made of thick plank wood. It was filled with bottles.

"What is it?" I said.

"Special brew!" he said.

"Eh?" I said.

"Our big brother is in the brewing business,

with Marky Taylor," he said. "We were right about that bit. They're selling the old rot-gut to Miles Sharry, and he's offloading it up the hotel to the tourists. It's old rot-gut!"

"That's illegal," I said.

Peter shrugged. "I know it is illegal, and you know it is illegal, and Sergeant Joe McDowell knows it is illegal . . . but that doesn't stop him buying a bottle or two off Miles at the hotel if he gets the chance!"

"But the Taylors were arrested last time . . . " I faltered.

"That was because old Taylor had no wit!" said Peter. "He was caught in Squirestown, trying to flog the stuff out of the boot of his car. He deserved to be caught! It isn't old Taylor this time, Miles Sharry made sure of that. He has Marky Taylor and our Baxter on the job, brewing up by moonlight on his own private still!"

"People die from drinking that!" I said.

"Not if it is brewed right," said Peter. "Don't worry, Miles has too much sense to let them make him any old poison."

"Baxter shouldn't be doing it!" I said.

"I don't suppose he has much choice," said Peter.

He was right there. Miles Sharry had him lock, stock and barrel. If Baxter wouldn't do his bit of home brewing for him, then he'd find somebody who would, and that somebody would likely end up with Baxter's job in the hotel bar as well . . . not that it was a *real* job, but it was the only job that was going, even a fool could see that.

"So that's where my twenty quid came from," Peter said.

I was relieved, in a funny way. The old poteen business was something I could put up with, even if I didn't like it. Anything was better than Baxter being a thief.

"We'd better hide the stuff away," I said.

We put the plank back in position on top of the hide. Peter carefully laid the sods on top, and then, when it was in position, he got the yard-brush and brushed carefully across, filling in the cracks, and last of all he put an old tin tray on top. We stamped up and down on it, to make it look firm like the rest of the floor.

"It's real good," I said. "You'd never guess it was there."

We left it, and walked back to the house.

Baxter had showed up again, still mad at me.

He was stomping round the kitchen, spitting teeth.

"Well?" he said. "Come to say you're sorry?"

I looked at Peter.

He shrugged.

"I'm sorry for what I said about you," I said. "But it was an honest mistake."

"That'll butter you no parsnips!" Baxter said. I could see he was still mad at me, and I began to get mad myself.

"Anyway," I said. "You are no better than you should be. What about all the stuff hidden away in the barn!"

That pulled him up short.

"You're too nosy for your own good, the pair of you!" he said, after a bit.

"You don't deny it, then?" I said. "You don't deny you've been making old rot-gut for Miles Sharry to poison people with!"

"What's the harm in it?" he said, uneasily.

"If it wasn't for our Dad I'd go and tell the police what you're at!" I said. "If I had my way you and Marky Taylor and Miles Sharry would all be locked up, and somebody could throw away the key."

"You can talk!" Baxter said, sharply. "What do you expect me to do?"

"Oh yes," I said. "Great. Whatever Miles Sharry says goes, because he has the money bags, and everybody round here knows what side their bread is buttered on."

"Right in one!" Baxter said, angrily.

"She is right, though, Baxter," Peter said.

Then Baxter did a terrible thing.

Peter's new pike rod was by the door.

Baxter picked it up and laid it across his knee. Then he snapped it.

"You git!" Peter said.

"Here," Baxter said, chucking the broken rod at him. "Take that and get out of my sight!"

For a moment I thought Peter was going to go

for him, and I was wondering what I could do to stop it, for they are both too strong for me, but I was saved because Peter just threw the rod down with a clatter, and then he belted out of the house, and away up the lane.

"I hope you are satisfied, Baxter Orr!" I said. I never thought I'd see our Baxter do a wicked thing like that.

Baxter used a bad word.

"You're a . . . a . . . a *louse*!" I said.

That pulled him up short.

"Yeah." he said. "Yeah, well, I'll get him another one."

"That won't undo the trouble," I said. I was nearly crying. I *would* have been crying, only I wouldn't give him the satisfaction. It was a mean bad thing to do to a person like Peter, even if he had been snooping and getting under Baxter's skin.

"Oh hell," Baxter said. "I didn't want all this, Annie. I didn't want it. But what am I supposed to do?"

"You're hopeless," I said.

He slumped down in my Dad's chair, by the kitchen table.

"Don't blame me," he said. "It's just that . . . there's all sorts going on, Annie. You don't know the half of what is happening."

"I know you have sold yourself to the Sharrys!" I said. "Miles and his money, and that one in her tight pants!"

"Keep Allie out of this," he said.

"She's making a fool of you, Baxter," I said. "She doesn't fancy you one bit."

"I know that!" he said.

"Oh yes?" I said. Then I told him about what she said to me, up at the Kominskis'. "So you needn't let on that you aren't carrying on with her behind her Dad's back for I know that you are!" I finished, triumphantly.

"You don't know," he said.

"What don't I know?" I said. "What don't I know that I can't see with my own two eyes?"

"I can't tell you," he said. "You'll just have to accept that there are things you don't know . . . reasons . . . there's a thing I have to do, Annie, and I can't tell anyone till it is done with. Till then, will you just lay off blackguarding the Sharrys. There's all sorts of trouble there, that you know nothing about."

"How can I know, if you won't tell me?"

He said nothing.

"What won't you tell me?" I insisted. "I've a right to know!"

"There's a thing I've got to do," he said, slowly. "And it is a thing I'm doing for Allie, because she asked me to. And I'm doing it because it is the right thing to do, *not* because she asked me. But I can't tell you what it is because I daren't tell anyone."

That took me up short.

"Don't you go doing whatever it is just

because she tells you to!" I said. "What are you, some sort of fool?"

"I've to do it anyway," he said. "It is too late for second thoughts now, for me or Allie. I've no way out."

And he would say no more.

12

It was nearly ten o'clock, and dusk was falling on the lake. Neither Peter nor my Dad had shown up, and Baxter was just hanging around the place. He had his anorak on, and he was out on the wall in front of the house, watchful.

I was up in my room. We'd had words about it, and he almost ordered me upstairs, though he wouldn't tell me why or what for.

"Early night for you, Annie!" he said.

"It's the summer holidays," I told him. "I don't need early nights for there is no school to go to."

"Tonight you're having one just the same," he said.

I thought I would argue it, and then I thought I wouldn't. Safer to let him think I was an innocent kid sent-off-to-bed, rather than somebody who was going to do her level best to stop old Allie Sharry's plan, whatever it was.

I went upstairs, anyway, leaving him in the kitchen, but I didn't just do that. I took a look in his room, for Allie Sharry's white shoulder-bag. I thought there might be something in it that would give me a clue to what was happening, but I couldn't find it.

Which meant there *was* something in it, or he wouldn't have hidden it! What could that be? Watching him waiting in the yard, looking out over our lake, I put my mind to work on it.

Baxter fancied Allie Sharry. Maybe Allie Sharry was mixed up in the IRA, and that was what all the secrecy was about. That was my first idea, but it didn't sound like the Sharrys. They're not that sort of people, and they're Protestants, anyway.

I thought a bit about what could be in the bag, and why there was all the fuss at Sharrys', with the hotel closed, and the police blocks and everything . . . though probably the police blocks were nothing to do with it. Police blocks are usual enough round our place these days with the trouble. Police blocks are usual, but closing down business for the day isn't especially for people like the Sharrys, who stay open no matter what!

Some trouble at the Sharrys', then.

And Allie Sharry's old face, and the way she talked to me . . . some trouble *she* was in.

Where would Baxter come into that?

Why would she make mystery appointments to see him, 'it's on for tonight', and pass him over her white bag and come down the house the way she had? She'd never been down round our house before, or at the Kominskis' . . .

There was one obvious answer, but I didn't believe it.

She was eloping with Baxter.

What about the bag, then? Why give him her white bag to hide?

Well, what goes in a bag . . . MONEY!

If they were going to elope, they'd need money, and Baxter had none, so it would have to come from Allie.

Where would Allie get it?

Would she *steal* it from her Dad's hotel, and never let on? Maybe she had done that, and Miles Sharry had found out it was missing but not who took it, and there was a whole row with the police called in. She'd taken the money and given it to Baxter and he was holding onto it, and 'It's on for tonight' meant he was to meet her, then they would do a skip to London or Dublin or someplace where her Dad couldn't find them.

Perhaps she'd told Baxter she'd elope with him, and then she wouldn't, she'd just dump him. That would be a Sharry-type thing to do!

Maybe she was eloping with the man she was with in Kominskis'. That would be great. She would buzz off with her fancy man and Baxter would be left to get all the blame for helping her and stealing the money, all because her sweet talk and her big eyes and her soft hair had him taken in.

My Dad might lose his job over it.

Could be it wasn't her at all. It was another of Miles' dodges! Drugs? I stopped at that one. If he wasn't above selling rot-gut from the Taylors, maybe he was on the drugs as well, and that was what all the police cars were about. There's been a lot in the papers about drug running in the country . . . would old Miles be in that too? Anything there was money in, he *could* be in on.

Baxter could go to prison, and my Dad could lose his job over it, and then we'd lose our house and there'd be nothing left.

I was getting really worked up about it when I heard the boat engine.

A boat had come creeping into the bay, low throttle, and was heading for our jetty.

Baxter came out of the barn, with Allie Sharry's white bag under his arm.

He headed off down the path.

I grabbed my anorak and my torch . . . for it was getting dark . . . and I struck off after him. I don't know what idea I had in my head, but I was hoping that someway I could stop him.

I'd been hoping that my Dad would come back, although it was a bit early for that, or Peter would show up, so that I could tell them what I was afraid of, and they would help me. But they hadn't come, and there was nobody else I could turn to. That's the trouble with living down Cow Lane with no neighbours but the Taylors and old Jackie, and no telephone either.

Baxter went by the path, taking his time, but I nuked off through the bushes.

I was down among the reeds by the landing stage when he reached it.

He went and stood on the end of it, waiting for the boat.

Allie Sharry hadn't even the decency to come herself.

There was a man in the boat. He had a balaclava on, and a muffler round his face, so I couldn't make out who he was. He was big and got-up to look tough in his outfit.

He called something to Baxter, and Baxter called back.

Then the man put an oar over the side, and poled her in. He wasn't very good at it.

Baxter got into the boat. He kept a firm grip on Allie Sharry's shoulder bag.

His face was dead white.

He looked frightened.

I didn't know why, and then suddenly I did.

The man in the boat had a gun.

He was pointing it at Baxter, and talking.

Baxter talked back at him.

Then the man put the gun down, on the seat between them.

I thought Baxter was going to go for it, but he didn't. He just sat where he was, clutching the bag.

The man started up the engine, and they chugged out of the bay, and round Taylors' point.

I was scared and I didn't know what to do.

Then I did.

I had to get help.

The only help there was likely to be was from the Taylors, and I didn't like going there, but I was past the point when what I liked or did not like doing came into it.

I was off down the lane as fast as I could go, but I couldn't go fast enough.

The boat was well out and passing Spike when I got to Taylors'. But it was dark. There was nobody there!

Just like old Marky and his Ma and Da to be out when I needed them.

Baxter was away in a boat with a man with a gun.

Kominskis' was the nearest help, and even the Kominiskis have no phone and no car. I could get Petra's bike and ride down to Bellaghery and . . .

I couldn't. It was no go.

I did the only thing I could do.

13

I was out in the night on the cold dark lake, with our big engine turned down to quarter throttle, and the Taylors' old leaky boat that I'd borrowed, chugging along.

I had to follow, and hope that there'd be another boat on the water, someone I could get to help me, who would know what to do.

There wasn't.

And the boat Baxter was in went *between* Spike and Woody, out into the main channel, so that I had to go out after it, there was no chance of hugging the lake shore and giving a shout to the Major or his holidaymakers, even if any of them had been about.

Even doing that I was in dead trouble.

If the man with the gun realised he was being followed . . .

That was why I kept the boat at quarter throttle, even though it meant I had to go slowly. I knew that with our big engine stuck on Taylor's leaky boat I had the power to overtake the other boat, if I needed to . . . but what good would it do? I couldn't tackle a man with a gun, and he would hear me coming a long way off, even if the dusk hit me.

What I did was *not* to head for the gap through Spike and Woody, but to make for the gap between Runey and Spike, which would bring me out downwater of the other boat, but far enough back not to be seen, especially if I kept into the side of the island. Then I thought the best I could do was to see where they were making for and follow, until I had a chance to make land, *if* I had a chance to make land, and get help.

I could hear the engine of the other boat phut-phutting across the water, and my big worry was that they would hear mine.

The only other thing I could think of to do was to flash my torch and hope somebody would see it and guess I needed help. There were two things wrong with that. One, I didn't know how to do SOS or those things, and two, I thought the other boat might see the flashes.

Then I worked out that the clever thing to do was to put myself in the boat so that my body was between them and the flashes. I did it, and I flashed my torch, but I hadn't much hope for it. Somebody *might* pick it out, *if* they were watching on the far side of the lake, but in the normal way nobody would be. The big hope was that the police would be nosing around the way they had most of the day . . . it wasn't a *very* big hope.

I brought my boat slowly up Runey, flashing all the way, and then I stopped flashing as I moved out into the space between the two islands, Runey and Spike. I was worried about that bit, because once I was clear of the side of Runey I thought they might be able to pick out the dark shape of my boat following them, even if they couldn't see the torch. What I did was to let them get further ahead, so that the angle where I could be seen was reduced, and then I upped the throttle a bit and went inside Woody Island and quickly up the lake, flashing away like mad at our side of the lake and counting on the mass of the island cutting off the engine sound. Just coming up to the end of Woody I put the torch down and cut the engine and let her run with the tide, hoping I could pick up a sighting of the other boat. Drifting round the Bailiff's rocks I thought I caught a glimpse of them, moving just wide of the Holy Island, rounding the Point and then turning back in. Then they in their turn were lost behind the land mass.

I upped throttle, with half a notion that I might make a run for Bellaghery pier, but it was too far away. By the time I got there, got help, and got back they'd be gone altogether!

I might have been all right, if I could have been sure that they would make a landfall on the island, *and stay there*. But if the other boat headed up the lake — *beyond* Holy Island — then they might make a landfall anywhere, on either side, or in one of the twisty bays or inlets.

There was nothing for it but to head after them, flashing the torch when I thought I could get away with it, and risking a bit of throttle as well. I headed straight up the inner channel, swinging directly left as I came out of the cover of Woody and the Bailiff's rocks. That gave me a wide angle, where I could see down the channel to Bellaghery, as far as I could see at all. The pier lights were just yellow pinpricks, far away I moved up channel, and wide round the end of Holy, torch off, throttle down, very slowly so I'd attract no attention.

On the main channel side of Holy I cut the engine altogether, and just drifted, peering into the darkness, at the old black island and the shapes of the trees and bushes and ruins there, with the round tower jutting above.

If they were on the island, the man with the gun would be keeping an eye for any trouble. My only chance was to pull in in the darkness, using the oars, and make the best landfall I could, then . . .

Then *what*?

I made my landfall, on the main channel side of the island, by the stepstone rocks, where I was able to tie the boat in under the bushes there, and get onto firm ground . . . if you can call an old marsh firm.

I got into the bushes, and then I had to scramble back again, after my torch.

Wouldn't you know! It was in the bilges of the Taylors' old leaky boat, in two inches of water.

I clicked it, but nothing happened.

Then I thought maybe they'd have something on board I could take with me, something to defend myself with . . . though I didn't fancy my chances. Nothing. Not a thing. Trust the Taylors not to have any kit on the boat. Not that a fishknife would have been much good . . . but it would have been something . . .

Would it?

Baxter had been dead right. I should have stayed out of it. I couldn't take on some gunman with only a fishknife.

What could I do?

I could try what they do in films. Get a stone and chuck it at the side of his head and knock him down and hope that Baxter would be quick enough to get the gun.

They get away with it in films and TV, but I knew that it wouldn't work on the island, in the darkness, for me.

I got a big stick, but it was more for company than protection, and then I started moving.

It was dark.

I tried not to think about the McSorleys' vault and all that, but I couldn't manage it altogether.

Who could, trying to ghost in between the trees, with the thought that out of the shadows at any moment might come a . . . I didn't like to think what might come!

I headed for the high point in the island, where the Round Tower is. You can't get up the Tower, for the door is kept locked . . . it's a green

metal door, one the Ancient Monuments people
put on, so the Government could keep it all to
themselves. That was the high ground, and
probably the best place to be, with my boat only
a short way behind me, so that I could belt back
to it, if I had to.

I got to the Tower.

Nothing.

No sign of life.

No *sound* of life.

Maybe the man with the gun had gone on
down the main channel, and I'd missed him and
lost Baxter and made a fool of myself and Baxter
would be dead before I had any chance to put it
right.

Or maybe not.

I was pretty well convinced I hadn't lost the
boat in the main channel, but suppose it had
gone in the rush channel, and worked down
towards the Bellaghery side, coming in amongst
the reeds on the *mainland*, not the island?

That was a facer!

If I'd lost the track, I'd lost the track . . . the
best thing seemed to be to go back to the boat
and run, full throttle, down to Bellaghery to
raise the alarm.

But if they *were* on the island . . . *somewhere* . . .
then cutting and running would be impossible,
because I'd have to put her up to full throttle
and the engine noise would give away what I
was up to. If the man was going to shoot Baxter,

he'd do it and be well away before I was anywhere near Bellaghery.

There isn't that much of Holy Island but there
are a lot of trees and reeds and old buildings, not
to mention the vault . . .

I couldn't make a run for it, until I was sure
the man with the gun wasn't *on* the island, that
was the decision I came up with.

I had to make sure.

That didn't mean searching the place, it was
simpler than that.

All I had to was work my way round the shore
line.

If the boat was there, they were there, and I'd
have to do whatever I could think of to do.

If the boat wasn't there, then they'd made for
the mainland, and I'd lost them. Then all I
could do was to get the alarm raised as soon as
possible.

I started off round the island, as quick as I
could go, threading my way in the dark, looking
for the boat.

It was down amongst the reeds, close to the tin
hut.

I stood looking at it in the darkness.

We were alone on the island. Baxter, and the
man with the gun, and me.

Annie Orr.

Maybe they were at the hut?

I worked my way up towards it in the dark.

Dead silent.

I took my heart in my hands and went in through the broken window, thinking I might find Baxter dead on the floor.

Nothing. Just rubbish and some old sacks.

I lifted the sacks.

Containers and things. Two containers, with stuff slopping about in them. Taylor's Home brew! I'd stumbled on the site of Miles Sharry's private distillery!

That gave me the first good idea I'd had.

I did it, quick as a flash.

That left me back at the gunman's boat, still not knowing which way to turn, and scared stiff of staying still because of what might happen, while at the same time I was scared to move for the like reason!

The man almost caught me.

I don't know where he came from. Out of the bushes, somewhere. He was big, that's about all I could see, for by that time I was down in the mud and praying.

He didn't come to the boat. He went on among the trees, and another one came behind him. I could hear them, and just about see their shapes, and the one sure thing I knew was that there was no way Annie Orr could stop big men like that by chucking stones, or hitting them with a stick.

I wouldn't even have dared to go after them, if it hadn't been for what happened next.

They came back through the trees, panting and cursing, and *dragging*.

They had somebody by the arms, and they weren't too fussy about what they were doing.

Baxter?

I just couldn't let myself think it was Baxter. If it was Baxter he was dead, or hurt.

They got clear of the bushes, and between them they heaved the other one up and humped him along.

All I could do was to follow them and hope they didn't get wise to me, and see if I could do something, somehow.

They didn't go far.

I watched them in, and I watched them out again, swinging the rusty door behind them, so that the squeak of it hurt.

Then they were lost in the darkness, heading towards the old church.

I knew what I had to do, but I didn't want to do it . . . no torch, or anything!

If there was one place above all the rest on that old island that I didn't want to go in, the place I was going to was it!

But I *had* to go, because of Baxter.

14

The McSorleys' vault.

The last McSorley was hung. Would he be in there, with the rest?

I just couldn't let myself think about that, because if I had, I'd never have been able to do it.

The old vault is built like a little house with a steep roof, and a barred door. I'd seen through the bars before, and seen the little narrow steps you could scarcely get a coffin down, to the chamber below. The McSorleys lie down there, though probably not the hung one. Just the ones that were buried in a decent way.

All in their coffins, in niches along the walls.

I came across the rocks, slow as slow.

No movement but me, as if I was the only one on the island, but I knew I wasn't.

The lock on the door was broken. I went down the damp steps into the ground, feeling my way against the clammy walls.

It was black at the bottom, in the burial chamber.

"Baxter?" I said.

There was no reply.

I put my hand out, groping, and my fingers ran along a kind of ledge.

I pulled my hand back, without touching anything. If I had touched one of the old dead McSorleys in their niches, hung or not, I'd have died there and then, standing up, on the spot.

I went forwards, an inch at a time, touching the *edges* of the ledges.

Then . . . a wall.

I felt up and down it, and my hand came away damp and slimy.

Nothing.

Obviously it was a big room, with ledges around the sides. I'd come along one side. I didn't like to think what was *on* the ledges . . .

I touched my way along the wall, to the corner, and I turned back . . . suppose back didn't bring me to the foot of the steps? I'd be in there with the old dead McSorleys for life!

Would anybody ever come and look?

Then the worst thing ever happened.

I *stood* on *somebody*!

And the somebody groaned.

I screamed and I screamed and I screamed.

I couldn't help myself screaming, but it was a weird thing. While I was doing it, I could *hear* myself screaming, and I wanted to stop me screaming, but the screaming just went on.

I was on the ground.

I don't know if I fainted, or what, but I was lying on somebody, and the somebody was warm.

113

Not an old dead body.

"Baxter?" I said.

I groped in the darkness, desperately, not even sure what end of the somebody I was at, and I found a head.

It was baldy!

It wasn't Baxter!

The head moved with my fingers on it, and then I felt something tied there, and my fingers were scrambling at the tie and it came away in my hands and the head groaned again. I nestled it . . . for it, or for me? I don't know which. It wasn't *dead*, that was the thing. It was alive, breathing, warm against me, and I wasn't alone.

I don't know how long I just sat there, feeling it breathe.

I'd gone cold.

I suppose it must have been the shock.

The next thing I heard was the scrape of the tomb door, and footsteps coming down the stone stairs in the darkness.

I hadn't even got my bit of wood.

A torch flashed in my eyes.

"Annie Orr!" a voice said.

It wasn't the man with the gun.

It was Sergeant Joe McDowell, and his arm was round me and we were both on the floor and I was up against him, sobbing my heart out.

Then there were more policemen, with guns and lights, and they were lifting up the one that I stood on.

114

"Never mind, Annie," Joe said. "Never mind. There there now, wee heart. You're all right."

"How about Miles?" one of the other policemen said.

Then I knew who it was!

Miles Sharry!

It was Miles Sharry I'd stood on, out cold on the floor of the McSorleys' tomb. Miles Sharry, with a great black bruise on his face and ropes round him, all trussed up like a chicken.

"Where's Baxter?" I said. "Oh Joe, where's Baxter?"

"Baxter?" Joe said. "Is it your Baxter?"

"Is he . . . is he dead? Did the man shoot him?" I said, all confused and frightened, for I hadn't an idea what was going on.

"That's who it is then," Joe said, and he shouted at the other policemen. "It's Baxter Orr did the delivery job! He's the one they're holding."

They took me up the steps. There was a lot of talking and shouting going on and one of the policemen had me in his arms. I was holding onto him like grim death and I kept asking him about Baxter, but no one would tell me.

There were policemen with rifles.

"Lie there against the wall, Annie, and don't move," the policeman told me.

"Baxter?" I said. "What about Baxter?"

He had to hold me down.

"I want Baxter," I said.

115

There was a man with a megaphone, up by the old church. He was shouting something, but I couldn't hear it.

"Tell me!" I said. "Will nobody tell me?"

"Stay still!" the policeman said. "Keep your head down."

"But . . ."

"Your brother's all right," he said. "He'll come to no harm. He'll come to no harm, Annie. But you'll do him no good if you get yourself shot."

There was someone shouting back from the ruined church.

"Tell me!" I said desperately.

"Your brother's all right," the policeman kept saying.

"No, he's not. Where is he?"

"He's up there," the policeman said. "In the church. With . . ."

"With who? Who's he with? What did Baxter do?"

I struggled to get free of him, but he pinned me down.

"Do you want yourself shot?" he said, shoving my face against his chest.

"Tell me!" I tried to say a third time, but I couldn't say it properly because his hand was half over my mouth. I nearly bit him!

He started whispering.

"Your brother's up there, at the church," he said. "The men who kidnapped Mr Sharry are with him. They're holding him. They'll let him go if we let them off the island. That's what they're saying."

Kidnapped.

Miles Sharry had been kidnapped. That was what it was all about. And Baxter . . .

"Baxter's not a kidnapper!" I said, knowing he couldn't be, not Baxter. Baxter would never do a thing like that.

"Sharry's daughter, Alexandra, made a deal," the policeman said. "The money for her Da. Your Baxter was just the delivery boy. He had the short end of the stick . . . and look where it has got him."

Allie Sharry's white bag . . . the bag with the money for the kidnappers!

"But . . ." I began.

"Hold it!" the policeman said. "Down!"

He pulled me down to the ground.

I screwed my head round, and I could just see what was happening, in the light of the torches.

There were four figures by the church door.

Three kidnappers and Baxter.

One of the men had a shotgun, and the gun was right up against the back of Baxter's head.

The man shouted something at the police, waving them back.

Then they started moving away from the church, with the torchlights following them.

I don't know how many police there were. They were about everywhere, with their guns

117

and their lights, but they weren't doing anything to save Baxter.

The policeman with the megaphone shouted out that nobody was to move.

I was hoping there'd be an ambush, and then hoping there *wouldn't* be, because if there was Baxter would be the first one shot.

The men moved towards the trees.

One of them had Allie Sharry's shoulder-bag wrapped round his wrist.

"They're taking Baxter!" I said.

"He'll be all right, love," the policeman said.

"They'll shoot him," I said, feeling . . . I don't know what I was feeling. Feeling just hopeless, because there was nothing I could do at all, and they had Baxter and nobody was going to help him.

"No, they'll not," the policeman said. "He's their only way off the island!"

With Baxter they could get off the island . . . without him there were enough policemen with guns about . . . but if anybody tried to get lucky and take a shot . . .

"What'll they do to him?" I said. "What'll they do?"

"Nobody's going to do anything," the policeman said. "Your brother won't get hurt. That's what we're here for!"

They were *there* all right . . . but what were they *doing*? They weren't doing anything but watching! What *could* they do?

118

Baxter wouldn't get hurt until the kidnappers got off the island. Then . . .

They were headed for their boat.

There was nothing anybody could do, but just watch.

They worked their way past the tin hut, and I was scared stiff that the police would start firing off, and Baxter would be killed . . . but nothing happened.

Then they were down at the reeds by their boat.

Two of them got in, and then Baxter, and then the man with the shotgun, pressed into the back of Baxter's neck.

"The boat," I said, suddenly remembering. "The old engine. I . . . "

"Shut up!" the policeman said, pushing me down.

They poled out.

Then one of the men got the drawstring, and started on the engine.

"I have the engine jiggered," I said, "She won't start! She . . . "

Then . . .

BOOM!

There was a roar and a flash and a gush of flame and smoke and . . .

Oh God! I'd blown up the boat, and I'd killed Baxter!

15

"I always said you'd be the death of me, Annie Orr, and you did your best!" said Baxter. "I'm a ruined man!"

He looked a ruin too, but just then I didn't mind. It was enough for me that he wasn't dead the way he might have been.

He was propped up in the hospital bed, with his arm broken and his leg in a funny sling thing with ropes and weights, so that it was stuck out in front of him.

"Look at me!" he said. "Wrecked!"

"I didn't mean to blow you up," I said, "I thought it was just the Taylors' old stuff. I thought if I watered the kidnappers' engine, the old boat wouldn't start and they'd be stranded out on the lake and it would hold them up and maybe they'd get caught and . . .

"And instead you blew the whole thing to pieces!" Baxter said.

"I didn't mean to!"

"It's as well you did it," Baxter said.

I didn't like to think about that. I didn't like to think what they would have done with Baxter once they had the boat clear of the island.

"Raw alcohol!" he said. "That'll be a lesson to

you. Never put raw alcohol near an engine."

"It wasn't my alcohol!" I said. "I didn't know it would do that!"

It was Baxter's fault, any road. Baxter and Marky making home brew out on the island in the darkness where they thought no one would be wise to it . . . Baxter and Marky for making the booze, and Miles Sharry for selling it under the counter in his hotel to the tourists.

"That old mix would fire your belly let alone blow up your engine!" Baxter said. "What about the Sergeant?"

"I expect the Sergeant has more on his mind than a bit of do-it-yourself brewing on an island," I said. "He has a few hospital cases to cope with."

That was true enough. The wonder was that nobody was killed, with pistols and shotguns and kidnapping and old boats blowing up, but nobody had been, and nobody had gone to a watery grave. Miles Sharry was back at the hotel, doing double the business with a bandage round his head and his picture on TV. The tourists were flocking in to see the Man-That-Got-Away! He wouldn't have been away, but for us, Baxter and me. Or maybe he would. Maybe the police would have got him even if Allie had played it by the book, and refused to hand over the ransom money, but Allie didn't.

Allie made up her mind to pay the ransom, and when one of the Sharrys gets an idea like that, that's it! It was Allie and her Dad *against* the police, as far as Allie was concerned.

So the police were left looking for Miles, and trying to keep an eye on Allie at the same time. They kept the news of the kidnap quiet, set up their roadblocks, and began searching around Bellaghery and the lakeside.

They must have been watching the lake with night-sights, like the soldiers use, my Dad says. Anyway, they spotted my flashing light and the toing and froing at the island, and made their move when we were all there; Baxter and the man who came for him, the other two kidnappers, Miles Sharry, and me. I could have wished they'd moved in a bit quicker!

The police were mad with Allie for going behind their backs and trying to pay the ransom, so the Sharry family weren't out of the woods yet, but I supposed they would learn to live with it.

People like the Sharrys usually come out on top.

That was what I felt about it, anyway, driving back to our house in Allie Sharry's car. You should have seen her. She was all dolled up, just as if nothing had happened, and I knew it wasn't for Baxter's benefit at the bedside visit, or mine.

I told her what I thought of her, because I thought she ought to know, and nobody else was going to tell her.

"You should never have used our Baxter," I

told her. "You had no right to get him to do a dangerous thing like that. He might have been killed."

So might I, I was thinking.

"There was nobody else I could trust like I'd trust Baxter," she said.

I was silent for a minute. Maybe she wasn't as bad as I'd been painting her. She really did like him, even if she didn't fancy him. And she'd trusted him, and believed in him, which was more than I had. She knew all along he was straight and honest, I was the one who called him a thief, when he wasn't.

"You could have done it yourself!" I said, still peeved at her.

She had her answer off pat. She couldn't do it because the police were watching her, and they were all over the place.

"You used him," I said. "You made sheeps' eyes at him and used him. You let on you fancied him."

"I did not," she said. "He's not my boyfriend, if that is what you're getting at, or likely to be. We just get on with each other, that's all."

"You know that," I said. "You know you'll go off and marry someone like your father, with hotels and bags of money. But does Baxter know it?"

"If he doesn't, I can't help it," she said.

"You used him," I said, repeating it so that she would get it into her head.

"Look," she said. "It was use Baxter, or have my Daddy killed on me. What would you have done?"

"I don't know," I said.

"And I'll tell you why Baxter did what he did," she said. "I'll tell you what you ought to know for yourself, already. He did what he did because he's a good person, not because he was going to get anything out of it."

"I do know that," I said.

"It's time you learned to trust people," she said. There was a spot of crimson in her cheek. She was really angry. "I just wish I had someone like Baxter for a brother, that's all."

I was still thinking about it when she dropped me back at our house.

Peter had the meal made, and we sat and had it, and I looked at my Dad. I would have done the same as Allie Sharry, if I had thought it was what was needed to save him. She was right! She probably loved old Miles the same way I love Dad. She wasn't mean or bad or trying to use anybody, she was just doing the best she could for the people she loved.

My Dad got up.

"I'm going for a dander by the lake," he said.

Something went *snap* inside me.

"I'm going with you!" I said.

He blinked at me.

"Peter's coming too," I said. "Aren't you, Peter. We'll go round to Runey and see if you can spot your old pike!"

And we did.

It was fine.

It was just fine.

We were down by the lake with the sun winking on it and I watched the pair of them and it made me fed up with myself for all the months and months I'd spent not trusting them, or anybody else, as if the whole world was in a conspiracy against me because my mother died.

If my Dad didn't tell me, he must have had his reasons.

"Listen to me," I said. "We're starting a new regime in this family! We're going to get this place all wound up again, and no more moping about, and no more arguments and going our own ways. We're all going to look after each other, and then we'll be fine."

"Is that one of your orders?" Peter said.

"Hairy git!" I told him.

We walked on round the lake, in the sunlight. We had all been like shadows, going on doing the things we had to do, with nothing new allowed to grow between us. Everything had been bottled up.

"You know what?" my Dad said.

"What?" I said.

"You're getting to be a grand girl," he said.

Also by Catherine Sefton

THE CAST-OFF

She used to call herself a 'free spirit', even at the tender age of eight. Now, at fifteen, Marie Logan is living in a squat with a group of misfits, having stormed out after years of family fights.

There had always been rows, according to Marie's next-door neighbour, Alice, though door-slamming and screaming weren't *her* family's scene at all – her father just quietly upped and left, leaving Mum drowning in vodka and Alice to pick up the pieces. Although the girls aren't even friends, Alice is pulled into the search for Marie, and through her we trace their compelling stories full circle, from Ireland to London.

Alice's account provides a powerful insight into the problem of personal responsibility for the lives of others.

EMER'S GHOST

From the moment Emer finds the old battered doll, buried for centuries in a ditch, she knows there's something special about it – particularly when it cries real tears! Then she comes face to face with its owner. But what does the ghost want? Emer has an extraordinary mystery to unravel – a mystery that leads to real danger and an astonishing discovery.

THE GHOST AND BERTIE BOGGIN

Notice: Beware of the Ghost . . .

Bertie Boggin is the smallest Boggin in a house full of Bogginses. With no one to play with and nothing to do, Bertie is sitting on the bin in the backyard when he sees the notice. And there in the coal-shed is the Ghost.

Bertie and the Ghost become best friends and have all sorts of interesting adventures together.

The Kidnapping of Suzie Q

Suzie Q and her mum are on a trip to the supermarket when their lives take a sudden and terrifying turn. A raid on the shop is bungled, and Suzie finds herself taken hostage. Her kidnappers turn out to be incompetent amateurs, a fact which makes them more dangerous, not less. Suzie has to draw upon all her resources and ingenuity, solely to survive.

This tense and dramatic novel examines, with sensitivity and insight, the impact such a traumatic event has on the lives of its victims.

STARRY NIGHT

What is going on? wonders Kathleen.
First there's a mysterious visitor; then
Mammy and Frank are both upset; and
later she finds Rose crying. Everyone else
seems to know what's wrong and
Kathleen is determined to find out for
herself. But when the full truth of the
family crisis is revealed, Kathleen realizes
she can never be quite the same person
again. All her innocent dreams – her 'starry
nights' – are about to be shattered.

Winner of the Other Award, this is the
first of three novels concerned with the
devastating effects of living in Northern
Ireland. *Frankie's Story* and *Beat of the
Drum* are also available.

'A full-to-bursting novel' – *The Times
Educational Supplement*